Making Callaloo in Detroit

"Reading *Making Callaloo in Detroit* is like arriving at an unexpectedly fabulous party, rich with sumptuousness and surprise, peppered with a guest list eclectic and bright. Lolita Hernandez leads us on a melodic journey that explores the stories of outsiders, as well as a mysterious magic that compels us to hold onto our oldest traditions even as we are pulled ahead into new and unknown worlds."

Dean Bakopoulos, author of
Please Don't Come Back from the Moon

"Besides Hernandez's skill with the voices of her characters, her celebration of the food of these cultures is nothing short of amazing, and her rendering of parties, fetes, impromptu dances, holidays, and songs makes for a joyous read."

Anne-Marie Oomen, author of *An American Map*
(Wayne State University Press, 2010)

"Lolita Hernandez pulls you entirely into her world before she spins her tales. In her writing, you can taste the callaloo, hear the calypso music, smell the air on a gloomy Detroit day, and hear the accents of her Trinidadian kin."

Angela P. Dodson, editorial consultant and former editor
for the *New York Times* and *Black Issues Book Review*

Making Callaloo
in Detroit

Making Callaloo
in Detroit

Stories by
LOLITA HERNANDEZ

WAYNE STATE UNIVERSITY PRESS | *Detroit*

18 17 16 15 14   5 4 3 2 1

ISBN 978-0-8143-3969-5 (paperback); ISBN 978-0-8143-3970-1 (ebook)

Library of Congress Control Number: 2013954618

∞

Designed and typeset by Charlie Sharp, Sharp Designs
Composed in Pona.

Publication of this book was made possible by a generous gift from The Meijer Foundation.

These stories have been previously published:
"Five Workers Report on How the Deal Really Went Down"; "No Puedo Bailar";
"Making Bakes"; "Sometimes You Leap; Sometimes You Fall";
"Making Callaloo"; "Over the Belle Isle Boundary."

For Puhks and Puhksie

Contents

Preface

I grew up eating callaloo as if it was daily fare in the city of Detroit, along with schtew chicken, pelau, sanchocho, and listening to all the calypso Lords, as well as Latin jazz master Tito Puente. How does that happen? Imagine dancing on the Bob-Lo boat to someone among us singing the latest calypso tune when the boat band isn't playing. Who here even knows about callaloo or buljol or bakes? Or wining up on Ole Years night? Or any of that stuff that happens when a few outsiders look at a new and strange world, wondering how to fit in and don't quite. I was thrilled back then to eat American food: fried chicken, pizza, real spaghetti. Is that American? But the taste of the food Mama served never left my mouth, my heart, my soul. My parents, both from Trinidad and Tobago, Mama by way of St. Vincent, were staunch island people. They never became naturalized Americans, mainly because Daddy wouldn't give up citizenship to where his navel string was buried. And they kept up their culture through food and all that happens around the meal.

These stories are not an attempt to capture my culture through food. I didn't try. This just happened. Call it gut memory. Stuff stuck in the craw, can't expel, still burping up the flavors of real peppa sauce, and my beloved bacalao buljol and bakes. Callaloo is a metaphor like no other for all of this. A stew of dasheen leaves, ochroe, and some kind of protein—crab or salt pork—and maybe some coconut, served over rice, or not. Callaloo is not for everyone; it is a deep dark-green slime of unidentifiable flavors, a trip to an unfamiliar bush, a blending of surprises. A trip to another world right here in the D.

Enjoy.

Making Callaloo
in Detroit

Making Buljol

The morning was gloomy, fuh so. By gloomy I mean a feeling yuh can't quite put yuh finger on, a creepy sadness, a sense that something isn't right. Yuh wake up feeling heavy, as if some kind of presence is trying push yuh back to the mattress and yuh have to fight in order to sit up, flop yuh feet over the side of the bed, and plant them on the floor. I did all that and felt exhausted, but I maneuvered my way to the kitchen to see if I could determine the weather. Maybe it was only me feeling gloomy. Maybe the day was really shaping up to be bright sun. One could always hope; after all, where there is life, there is hope. My bedroom has a window, but in truth I have so much junk in there and heavy curtains that I can never gauge the day from the bedroom, which faces the front. I could well go to the little living room just on the other side of my bedroom wall and push aside the drapes and open up the blinds, but that's too much for early morning, and plus my disheveled self would be apparent to the street in case some nosy neighbors were peeping my way. So to make a decision about weather and its relation to my mood, I have to go to the back porch off the kitchen. It's there that I determine if the world is still around and figure out what the day is going to be like.

In truth, the porch is as cluttered as the bedroom. The main problem is the newspapers accumulating since before BC, yellow and looking as if they could spontaneously combust, even with winter sun. Next thing is the set of boxes and boxes of rags I keep if in case I finally begin to sew again. They're not rags, yuh know, but nice scraps of material; I could make nice dresses and so on with them. But these days, I don't know, I don't feel to do all that.

When I opened the door leading to the back porch of my second-floor flat, the heat hit my face; no matter, it's always hot back here, even in the dead of winter. I could go out on the porch naked and plop myself on the couch and not feel any kind of chill. This morning I could well see how gray it was outside. Umhum, this could be one of those Detroit days; yuh know it isn't winter or summer, but yuh not quite sure if it is spring or fall because in this neck of the woods sometimes spring and fall look the same. If not for the calendar, yuh could be as hopeful in September as in May. Or as gloomy. The leaves on the ground could be left over from the previous fall once the snow clears, or it could be fall already and the leaves freshly on the ground announcing winter coming. The smell test was the only way to really know about the day. So I rotated the handle that worked one of two window slats that could open and took a sniff. Oh yes, this would be a gloomy day. The air was too heavy and full of rain, even for spring. To besides, if I moved my nose one way, the air was cold, and the other way, the air was warm. This was instability at its height.

But I lingered by the window with the cool breeze slipping in. The air was heavy but fresh. I glanced around the porch at the old flowery couch and side table. It was my favorite place to sit and meditate on the complications of life. Sometimes I would flip through the stack of *Life* magazines I've been collecting ever since I arrived in the country. Hmmm, I must have reached to 1967; I see pictures of the riots on the cover of the magazine on top. Oh boy, I wanted to return home when that thing broke out here, but what for? What would I do there? At least now I can sit on the couch for hours watching over the yard and nobody can bother me. In winter I can count snowflakes or get lost in their glistening or watch at how ice hangs on the cherry and plum trees in the yard. Once that is over I can find myself in full hope of spring. Yes, it sounds corny, but spring was always wonderful from that back porch. Summer was super stifling, sometimes I could scarcely breathe because only two slats opened, and like I said they could only open a little. But spring was fresh and nice, provided winter was not lingering on its tail. Little green things would begin to pop through the soil. I would immerse muhself in the miracle of life and growth and regeneration and all of that. The owner of the house would be out there in good weather, weeding or planting or putting out yard curios to make the place look nice. She was the real herald of spring. When she was out, yuh knew the weather was changing; all the nastiness of winter was gone: snow, cold, frost. To tell yuh the truth, until I would see her out picking weeds and so on, I never believed the weatherman. The landlady was from the islands like us, a different one, but she had the green thumb and grew mint, sunflowers, bleeding hearts, all kind of flowers to make the place look almost like the tropics. She had a special connection with nature; she was in tune with the universe in a way I was not. But she gave me permission to pick as much mint as I wanted and flowers, too. I took the permission as an invitation to join her in special relations with nature and the universe and her cat, another manifestation of nature. It patrolled the garden as if guarding all the greenery and colors its mistress generated. The cat never climbed the fence to run off or disturbed the garden. It just existed there. I was convinced about the magic of this woman mainly because of the cat. But I'm not too particular for mint in my ice tea. I find that I put too much sugar to compensate for the mint, which is not good for my health or my figure. And I didn't like the idea of picking the woman's flowers. So I would sit on the porch with the slats open, inhaling the mint and enjoying the colors below. And I would watch the cat.

But this morning there was no time to engage in philosophical nonsense and digressions about weather and gardens of mint and the life of a cat. My cousin once or twice removed, however you categorize the family tree, called me early all jittery, telling me to get to the hospital quick. Tings dohn look good, gyul. He not opening his eyes. His breathing is shallow and he pissing on himself. O lorse, gyul, he de lahs a dat set. All dem dat came during de war. I dohn think yuh even know everyting. Dey was one helluva crazy assemblage of folks, yuh know. To dis day, I can't figure out all de ins and outs a dem. But no mind. If he goes, is me an two a muh first cousins on top. An den you come next. So, hurry wit some buljol. If anyting can revive him, is dat. I on muh way to de hospital.

There are so few of us here: a cousin twice or three times removed or even someone who lived over there down the road from a cousin four or five times removed from a neighbor of someone else's cousin becomes close family. But she is my family fuh sure once or twice removed. Her mother and mine grew up together in the same family constellation. She always looks out for me. I always look out for her. But I am not so totally ting up, or as we would say, fahfusiated, with all them that I am at their beck and call. They are so full of commesse over here. I don't know if it's the air in this damn city or the politics in this country, too much crazy ideas about who is who and what is what. But, as I say, she is my family, fuh sure. She looks out for me; I look out for her. Back in the north corner of the porch I keep a collection of photos from home, with a chair next to it where I can sit to ponder the family, all of them, at my leisure. When this blows over, I'm going to fix myself a nice cool drink and study their faces again. Maybe he's in there.

Not long after the phone call, the landlady climbed up the back stairs and knocked gently on the door. Evidently, my cousin had called her as well to make sure I fully got up and moved to make the buljol. She said through the door, everything OK? Yuh get de call from yuh cousin? Yuh need any help?

No, Mum. Everything is under control.

Yuh need a ride?

No, Mum. De car working fine. I can make it.

I'm here fuh yuh, gyul. Yuh need help, let me know.

Thank yuh, Mum. I appreciate yuh concern. I'll be OK and I'll let yuh know about everyting as soon as I reach by de hospital.

OK.

So I rushed into the kitchen, not quite awake, one half of my brain thinking about how I was going to pull off this buljol, the other half trying to figure out what I was going to wear, because I could speculate about the weather, but sticking yuh head out the window doesn't give yuh much of a real idea about temperature once yuh body hits the total environment. And no matter what, I can't stand cold. So even a slight drop in temperature makes muh joints ache and I begin cursing this place and wondering why I am here. But here I am in this stinking temperamental city and it could well be too cold out there for muh taste. The other thing is, maybe I should divide the brain into three, because truth is, the car wasn't functioning so well. I think the exhaust or something was not working properly. The car was making a lot of noise and a good bit of black smoke was coming out the rear end.

No mind, I had to get this show on the road, do my part, get some buljol to the hospital. I couldn't even begin to worry about whether or not they would allow me to bring the food in. What if they had him on some special diet? What if he couldn't tolerate the onions or green peppers or, o lorse, peppa sauce? O yes, that's what she meant. Buljol was plenty more powerful medicine than whatever they had dripping into him. So I shuffled everything around in the refrigerator, hoping to find enough codfish to fix up a respectable buljol. O ho, I found some. According to her, no time to waste. But first thing first; I must take the salt out the bacalao. So I fumbled around and found the little enamel pan with the flowers on it that I always use for my buljol. It would be a sacrilege to use anything else. This is the pan I grew up with Mummy making the buljol. I dohn know any other way to make it. And really, we were the ones to make it. So I come by it honestly. Mummy left me the pan and I make the buljol these days. So I grabbed the saltfish from a corner way in the back of the refrigerator. I want to say the size of the fish was about the length from the tip of my middle finger to the middle of my hand, just at the point where the thumb joins. That's a fair amount, considering the price for real bacalao. So I threw the bacalao and some cold water in the flowered pan. Saltfish was now in its first soak. While it was soaking, luckily I found a half tomato and some onion and, of course, I always have the olive oil. Things were looking good. What de arse, no green pepper, only a little tip of a red bell pepper? This will have to do. If I drop in a pinch of peppa sauce, he'll never know the difference. I was moving around the kitchen flough flough. I could barely catch my breath; I could scarcely think. But I had to get this batch of buljol together in a hurry.

Truth is I was too focused to even worry about hurry. I've made bad buljol before. This may sound unbelievable, but yes. I can't say I'm ashamed of myself, just that things don't always work out in life, no matter how hard yuh try. Like when I was working in the office at the university. The first thing I learned from Mummy, *Take yuh father heart and push forward.* Because that job was hard as hell for me. I didn't like the way the people looked down on me. They talked to me as if I was chupid. Then I went to work as a waitress at a so-so restaurant. Let me tell yuh, I wasn't too good at that, either. I didn't like the attitude of the customers and the people in the kitchen. Especially I didn't like the way the owner would look at me. I was a little younger and slimmer in those days. Not so long ago, but still I was more appealing. Not to say I can't turn an eye now, but when yuh younger like that and the hips are more in line with the waist and the belly doesn't stick out too much and the breasts sit up high. Yuh know, the men like yuh. I never know how to handle any of that. Mummy wasn't too good at explaining these things and the others in the family weren't any better. Yuh would hear a comment or two about dis and dat, but mostly yuh had to figure these things out for yuhself. These days I keep to muhself because I don't want to be bothered with too much confusion, commesse. To me commesse is all them with their various interpretations of dis, dat, and everyting else about this blasted city that they fancy themselves knowing so much about but they ent know nothing about it and always are trying to tell me as if they are so knowledgeable. Cheups, that's all I have to say. They don't know nothing.

Music, even music they would try to tell me about. Like I gon wine myself up in this city as if I was in de damn bush back where dey come from. Cheups again, right? Listen, even he tell me one day about a song he was hearing on the radio. Oh gosh, one big grin on his face, excuse me, what an old arse man like him know about "Sittin here la la, Waitin for my Ya Ya"?

Getting back to the occasional problems with my buljol—this is it; sometimes in preparation I don't take out enough salt, sometimes too much. Now and again I can't afford the good bacalao, so I go down to the Puerto Rican market and get pollock. Then I have to work my tail off to get the saltfish nice and flaky and tasting like something that could pass for a good buljol. Yuh judged by how you cook with dese people. So those are the times I can't serve the dish any ole how. I have to make nice bake—I prefer fry bakes—get a perfect zaboca—I go over by the Puerto Rican store for that—put in the right amount of peppa sauce, and so on. Oh, and make a nice Lipton tea.

First soak over. I pour off the water and I mash up the fish by hand. This is the secret weapon in my buljol. I think it helps spread the flavor of the other ingredients, giving more surface for the peppa sauce and the olive oil to soak in. Also, for quick desalting, flaking helps. So after the first set of cold water and the first set of flaking, I added more cold water. But not before tasting the fish to see how it was progressing with the desalting. Little bit more to go. If I'm lucky I could get away with only two sets of water. And as luck would have it, this was the good bacalao, not pollock. So it was nice and soft already. Mummy would always soak in cold water. Others boil the saltfish, but not Mummy. She had a process, a way to engage with the fish. Like with everything she cooked. She was slow and thorough. I began chopping the onion, tomato, and bell pepper, thinking about how she used to prepare the fish. I do mine just like hers, except for the occasional problems with quality and desalting too fast or too much. Otherwise, I have to say I make a damn good buljol, which is why I received the call this morning for my recipe to bring him back to life. Mummy would be proud of me. That kind of call. My buljol in demand to save his life. For that reason I eyeballed how much ingredients I might need for the amount of saltfish. But I took the precaution of not mixing the ingredients together just in case I needed to adjust portions to suit. It needed to be perfect.

OK next problem, as I mentioned the bakes, did I have enough time to make some, even a quick roast bake? I had to think for a minute to figure this one out. I could go by the Mexican bakery to get a nice hops bread, dem does call it pan bolillo, and that would do just as good as a bake, and I wouldn't have to get myself even more nervous than I already was. I could even have enough time for a quick wash-up while the saltfish was in second soak.

So that was the plan I settled on: wash-up during the second soak, make the buljol, and then make a hops stop at La Gloria. Then the hospital.

I was feeling it. I got into the full rhythm of the soaking, mashing, and making, the wash-up coming next and then hops stop. O Sittin here la la, waitin for my Ya Ya, ahm, ahm. Look, it's only natural I would begin to focus on him and the Ya Ya song. I was making buljol to save his life, and to tell the truth I hardly knew him except for one Sunday afternoon when we found ourselves, just the two of us, in the front room of his house, while his wife and all dem, including the cousin twice removed were in the kitchen cooking.

He was sitting in a fancy chair on one side of the fireplace; I was sitting in an equally fancy chair on the other side. The front room was large so we were far from each other. But since it was only the two of us, I felt funny, yuh know. He was hunched in the chair and grinning at me strange. In the few years I had been in the States and knowing him and the rest of dat set, I had never said more than two words to him, and here we were sitting across from each other in front of a fireplace and he was grinning. All of a sudden he said, You know what song I get a kick out of?

No, Uncle. He wasn't really my uncle unless it was five times removed, but he was plenty older, so of course I had to address him as uncle.

And he began singing, Sitting here la la, waiting for my Ya Ya, ahum. Sitting here la la, waiting for my Ya Ya, hum hum. By this time his eyes were closed and I saw him slip something into his mouth and begin chewing. I thought it was a piece of candy or maybe some tobacco. I'm not sure if I knew that he chewed tobacco. But who knows; the whole thing freaked me out. He asked me if I knew the song. I had vaguely heard of it. To tell you the truth, I wasn't too particular for the American music.

All in a sudden I remembered that my cousin told me he chewed dimes. Maybe that was what he put in his mouth that day he was waiting for Ya Ya. Come to think of it, I never saw him eat anything, not food, not tobacco, not a dime, not a nickel, not even a penny. For sure, not buljol or any food that we would gather to eat on Sundays at his house, which was more his wife's house and he was just there because he didn't join us to share food or laugh or gossip or any of the things that happened when the clan two-three-four-five times removed would gather on a Sunday, come rain or shine. Even on cold days we would gather. They had a splendid house, large, full of pretty furniture, rich looking, not like anything any of us had since coming to this country. Sometimes I felt as if by going over there to share food, we would be sharing their wealth. What did he do? How did they have so much? She didn't work. So where did the money come from? I never thought about that. No one said a word about that. For a family full of commesse like ours, why didn't we gossip about that somewhere else? Then I realized that they probably did, all dem only two maybe three removed. But I was too far out on the lineage and dey probably didn't include me; plus, I was too young at the time.

But I don't care who says what about what or who or how much dimes he supposedly ate or how much Ya Ya and la la he was experiencing ever in his life, which of course, I have no way of knowing about the extent of that, how much la la he was in while waiting for Ya Ya (and I have to assume Ya Ya was a she she), and maybe there was some district down the road or even one he lived in over there that was close to the sound or concept of la la, maybe la la was over there, and over here was something hard sounding, or maybe la la was in his mind. Maybe the Ya Ya singer was reminding him of all that over there. Maybe he knew the guy. No matter what, I never once, except for that afternoon when he sang Sitting here la la Waiting for my Ya Ya to me, I never once saw him put anything in his mouth. That was the only time and I don't know what passed through his lips. But for sure I never saw one drop of food. I never saw a flake of bacalao. So what make muh cousin, the one who called me this morning, think that buljol would save him? What, she believe in magic? Maybe so. Wit dese people all yuh can do is go wit de flow. Dey say buljol, you say right now. So right now it is. What de hell. I'm in la la and I'm de Ya Ya waiting for this fuckin bacalawow to finish wit de salto. O ho. All in a sudden I stopped so dead in the middle of de kitchen wondering what de hell was going on. Yuh find yuhself singing some chupidee song some chupidee old man sang years ago and now he is dying, pissing on himself and I'm here wit codfish and peppa sauce trying to revive him. What kind of crazy world is dis atall. Maybe I should put some dimes in the buljol. Why not. Maybe I should put a little Ya Ya in dere. Aahaaaa.

Ya Ya in de buljol waiting for some la la, ahumm. Sittin in de buljol waiting for some Ya Ya. Ahummm. OK OK, so I wine up from one side of de kitchen to de next feeling in perfect la la putting a touch a Ya Ya, in song mind you. And I must say everything came out perfect, yes, the buljol was one of muh best, even with the red bell pepper. You see the secret of this one was deee peppa sauce. It was the most supreme batch ever in my fairly young life. Oh yes, that peppa sauce had been soaking up every drop of sun it could for the past few weeks. True, no tropical sun was available, but I had the jars on the most hot sun window in the house and as the weather wasn't too cold, the peppa sauce was maturing nicely and could well offset the red pepper, which, in truth, is too sweet for a proper buljol. But let me back up for a moment to before assembling the buljol. That is when the devil entered my body.

Who knows where he came from, maybe la la. I found myself laughing without end. Then I went to my purse and rummaged around until I found a dime, one single dime. I never tasted one. Who in the hell puts dutty money in de mouth? Not me. But I figured, if I bring dis buljol to the hospital and if dey let me in wit it and if dey can get him to eat it, then maybe the taste of de dime would revive him. What dime taste like? Silver? Maybe silver has nutrients? Why not try? Maybe dime has more nutrients den fish. I wasn't thinking anyone in de hospital room would eat de buljol anyway. Everyone would be so upset and worried about if he would survive and what that would mean for de family over here in dis stinking city. What de arse, who gives a shit about stinking Detroit? Why are we here anyway? After all, dis ain't no la la over here. Hump.

So, in the dime went as the first ingredient that hit the flakes. In de meantime I'm signing over and over de only few words I knew of the song. Those were de only words I knew back then and dey are de same words I was singing right then over de bacalao. You see how it works? I learned them from him, because to tell you truth, when he began singing de song I well remembered the tune but not de words. I dohn always understand the language here. But now . . .

So in went de dime, then de onion, red pepper, tomato, peppa sauce, and I give de concoction one good stir. Then I gave it the sniff test; Mummy always said to smell de food when seasoning and before serving. De damn buljol smelled like de best I ever make. Dis last of dat set ent going anywhere, not today, not with this saltfish. So, now I had plenty of time to wash muhself off, make hops stop, and head to de hospital because I well knew he would be in some kind of la la and I was bound to make it in time.

Process Server

Smack dab in the middle of the block sat the three old women, like queens reigning from sturdy outdoor rattan thrones. They were not quite at the grizzled stage, meaning too arthritic to move about much, but each had a few hairs jutting from her chin and plenty of mouth to issue orders in the most lyrical cadences imaginable of their respective mother tongues. Move that here, plant that there, put the red, white, and blue impatiens over yonder. They took turns directing the horseman—imagine the block having a horseman—the teenagers, the young mothers and fathers, and any little ones who toddled past them. They were the lucky old timers who managed to survive because of attention from their respective families and/or neighbors and pure cussed stubbornness.

Maria Vitale, who had been a widow for many years, had lived the longest on the block, bar none. Some said that she sat down and the block grew up around her. Maria had been widowed for so long that she no longer had a story to tell about her husband. She had been there for so long that no one even speculated about who he was or how she got there with him. Maria was just a presence gradually discovered as those moving into the neighborhood began looking around and wondering about the short, stocky woman who peered out from her lacy windows or porch on good days and waved at everyone passing by. Maria refused to leave the neighborhood to live with her son, a successful contractor in the suburbs. Where Imma go? she would say to her son. I miei amici sono qui. I feel good here. I not moving. Solo per la morte.

Those were also the sentiments of Eva Lukow, a woman who years ago chose to stay in the States when her German husband returned to his homeland, leaving her with two daughters, Angelika and Brigitte. Her husband had preceded the girls and her to the States in the first place in order to get a job and a place for them to live here because things were tough over there after the war. When she arrived in the States with the girls, things went along OK for a while until she realized that her husband had become moody, sullen, and was beginning to speak harshly to her. He slapped her a few times, causing the girls to tremble in the corner and cry. She tried to talk to him. What else can you do when you are alone in a strange country with a man who was growing stranger with it? Finally, he blew up at life one day and left. Weeks later she received a letter from overseas saying that he had found a job with his cousin. He begged her to return to Germany with the girls. But she wouldn't. She didn't trust him anymore; her feelings had been hurt. In the weeks after her husband's departure, she began to immerse herself in the neighborhood and discovered that she liked the people around her, including Maria Vitale, with whose help she was able to find work at an Italian restaurant. A teenage girl across the way came every morning to take her girls to the school a few blocks away and bring them home at the end of the day. Eventually, both of the girls went to Germany when they reached of age to search for their father. They never returned to the States.

Ola Mae Hendrik was the last of the three to arrive on the block and the luckiest, for she lived with her daughter, son-in-law, and their children. She arrived from Athens, Georgia, Limestone County, the home of sweet iced tea. You know how every community or family has a seer? Someone who can sense things when everyone else is wrapped up in day-to-day problems? Someone who has a direct connect with forces that operate between raindrops and heat waves? That was Ola Mae Hendrik, better known as Granny, so respected for her sixth sense that individuals and families regularly sought her advice on delicate matters, from engagements to pregnancies and from divorces to deaths. Having dealt with all of life's major issues, especially coming from the South, Granny was like a book of knowledge, a resource for the neighborhood. If you wanted to be born again or live or die, you went to Granny for advice. If you wanted to love or figure out what went wrong with love, you went to Granny. You went to Granny for some advice on almost anything, except hating. Granny wasn't the type to hate. There was always a way to move past hate. Also, Granny never cooked. So there was no point going to her for advice on that. It's not that Granny was too old to cook at this point. You could understand that, but Granny *never* cooked. She couldn't stand it. Never had the patience for cornbread, greens, and whatever constituted Georgian fare, except she could make sweet tea like no other. Another thing about Granny: she loved to pick cotton in her day. And on this day she loved to order folks around about how to garden because that was where her true talent lay.

The day was caught between the end of spring and the promise of summer, a kind of sunny but cool that brought folks out to work in their gardens and to chat about how horrible the winter had been, but finally things were warming up. One or two mentioned the *Farmer's Almanac* and predictions of real serious heat this summer. That brought distressed looks from a few older residents, including Maria and Eva, who both lived alone, with only air conditioning units in their bedrooms or living rooms to try and cool their homes. Worse yet, fans that did no more than move heat around. Some had a combination of fans and small A/C units, with the fans strategically placed to distribute the cool air through other parts of the house, for example, from living room to bedroom or vice versa. Most likely the older residents would opt to have the A/C unit in the bedroom, because that's where they spent the most time, and then have a couple of fans blowing the A/C air out to other parts of the house, depending on the layout of the place. For the younger families, a single A/C unit might be placed in the living room, leading to huddles of parents and children sleeping there, with a few fans in other places. Problem was that A/C pulls current, and that means high electrical bills. It was a no-win situation for most of the older folks. But, frankly, that was how it was for most of those out there weeding and planting on Memorial Day weekend—whether small A/C units and/or fans—but the younger ones were better able to work around this humble arrangement. Back in the day, you could sleep on your front porch when nights were hot; you could catch a cool breeze now and again and no one bothered you because everyone was out there, believe it or not; if a criminal tried to mess with anyone, everyone heard and was already on the porch ready to spring into action. The only disturbance was snoring, especially from the older, beefy workers who had to get up early and hit the clock. They snored loud as the machinery they would be facing soon enough when the moon descended and the sun peeked up from the east. The snores alone kept away what was mostly petty thievery back then, like stealing something off the car, or what else? What else was there to take? What is there to take now? A TV? We have TVs today about the same relative market value as then; so what is the difference? The difference is now you're not safe in your own home, even with bars on the windows, unless you have a big dog and/or a gun. Forget about sleeping on the porch. The young folks could manage big dogs and guns, but the older folks in that area had to rely on big-dog barking to tumble over their way and maybe confuse a criminal, and guns were too much for them, the idea of killing someone. Sometimes aging makes you doltish and slow to figure out how to survive Mother Nature and the realities of urban living, in the heart of the city where you shouldn't have to worry about being alone and battling elements. But once you're inside your brick or wood housing tomb, you could be alone and undiscovered for days if something goes wrong and neighbors don't notice your absence until . . .

But this was one of those renewing and loving days among folks, who were like family—they had all been there long enough together. Even the younger ones with their young school-aged children felt as if they had grown up there, with relatively perfect strangers becoming grandmothers and grandfathers and aunts and uncles to their families. So there was a sense of commitment to each other that develops after many times of communal planting or snow shoveling or leaf gathering. Or neighborhood summer parties when the street would be closed off and tables of food specialties dotted the sidewalks, along with the garage sale where neighbors recycled their junk to another and another's became someone else's. Few outside the community knew of these summer events; few tasted the fried chicken, potato salad, macaroni and cheese, tamales, lemonade, seven-layer salad, cheesecake, or anise-laden biscotti that defined the neighborhood as a gourmet center.

And the dogs were as much a part of the scene as the children, each known by name and each respected for its contribution to the security and emotional well-being of the community. Even the yippy-yappy ones; at least their barks could alert.

The day was continuing as normal for the seasonal transition with marigolds beginning to edge the sunny portions of gardens and impatiens the shady areas, along with hostas and pachysandras. Teenagers raked up refugee leaves from last fall that hadn't managed to mulch into the rich soil that claimed the neighborhood. Lucky for all of them, the soil was deep and black and allowed gardens to grow wonderfully, especially since one of the neighbors had a friend with a real farm miles from the city. He would take his pickup truck and his two strapping sons out there every early spring and gather manure, which he deposited strategically throughout the block for all to access. In his day, he was a horseman, believe it or not, even in the city after he moved up from the South. He laughingly used to say that he was from Threepulo, just below Tupelo, Mississippi. He was a horseman back then and managed to keep it up when he settled in Detroit and began making some of that long money in the Cadillac plant.

His Threepulo memories with their horses stayed in his heart, and as soon as he could—given that he had a wife from Tupelo, believe it or not, who bore him two sons, obedient and calm boys who didn't get caught up in the street nonsense that Detroit had to offer, as well as a daughter who was brilliant and college bound—he acquired a horse from a guy who worked on second shift. He also made arrangements to board the horse at the man's stables and soon enough became involved in the Cadillac Black Horsemen's Club. Plenty of horsepower there that probably accounted for his sons being so calm, because they took up horse riding and associating with the club members in almost weekly excursions to the stables on the outskirts of the city. The girl took up books.

So it was the trio of the horseman and his sons who contributed nourishment to the soil of the community, as well as a sense of manly purpose in a positive and gentlemanly way that made all feel secure and focused. This particular day was not a party day, the kind when neighbors cackled loudly and hand slapped and displayed enormous amounts of gaiety at every twist and turn when everything was funny and anything that fell out of anyone's mouth was cause for laughter, that good old loud, guffawing kind that clears the lungs and frees the nostrils from winter's constraints, the mucous from colds and lack of humidity accompanied by high heating bills that did little to relieve frozen body joints, especially the knees, shoulders, and arthritic fingers. Backs, too, sometimes, and necks. This was a hardworking day in preparation for fêtes later in the season; this day was full of dirty hands and bent backs, simple garden tools, and deep cooperation with instructions from older, more experienced green-thumbed souls, like the three older ladies. The neighborhood was early on in its work, but already the man who had the most grilling expertise, the one who could, in the vernacular of the city, throw down when it came to bar-b-q and so on (don't talk about his baked beans), well he was firing up the grill, getting it ready for the traditional hot dogs on the first day of planting.

Everyone was in place: teens raking leaves, other teens moving manure to designated spots, the horseman regally patrolling by foot as if on horse, worker bees receiving instructions from the elders about tools to use and where to station themselves for maximum efficiency because the crew expected to finish close to mid-afternoon and chomp on the best hot dogs in the—let's say it—world. Detroit is the epicenter of hot dogs, and there they were with the main griller man. He was originally from Monterrey, Mexico, having arrived in Detroit years ago as a young boy with his family. He followed his father into work at the Rouge. He also learned to grill from his father. One Saturday each summer the community designated "fajita day." Everyone chipped in to buy the meat, and the main griller man and his family would spend the eve of the day preparing for the day of. Neighbors brought sides and beer.

Gourmet food folks, gourmet grill man, gourmet hot dogs. Now this was a recipe for intense communal gardening. You might think that folks gardened collectively for love of color in the summer. But it was the grill man and the hot dogs that motivated the beginning of the season and the need to get the manure in ground. Late-season weeding and maintenance activity would require a different set of motivations. But this day was about hot dogs and the first collective time in the new fresh air, the beginning of new life, the herald of warmth, and all that crazy and fabulous hope for a few months of relaxed and civilized living.

The neighborhood people were loaded with a special history of cooking, which inspired the mélange, the cultural mix, the wonderful flights of flavors, the freedom to do whatever spice and not feel locked into specifics. Maria was among the talented cooks, especially the most marvelous spaghettis imaginable, parmigiana concoctions from her home deep in the mountains of southern Italy and biscottis that eventually introduced the neighborhood to anise and to her. She was especially fond of anise as a tasty aid to digestion and would make biscottis throughout the year, not just at Christmas. For her, biscottis were the perfect way to top off a meal any time of the year. And the perfect way to begin a special circle of friendship, which is what happened on a steamy summer evening not long after Granny's arrival in the neighborhood when, in Maria's opinion, she had created the most magical biscottis ever.

Ola Mae, who lived two doors down from Maria, was an anomaly, not a cooking talent. One day, early on her arrival to Detroit, she decided to take a short walk to survey her new territory. She was strong enough to walk the entire block, and she was determined to do so on her own, as she was still smarting from her daughter and son-in-law's insistence that she relocate north with them. They just about had to pluck her out of Athens, where she was living by herself in a remote area. She wasn't entirely thrilled to be in the North and in a household full of children, three in all, but they were well behaved and tolerable. She loved her son-in-law. Her daughter got on her nerves with her bossiness. But she loved her, too. Of course.

So, Ola Mae edged down the steps of her daughter's modest brick home and turned left to head north toward the church just at the beginning of the other block across the side street, no more than three-quarters of a block away from her new home. She had spied it on the way in and took note. Her daughter and son-in-law no longer attended church, so they knew nothing about the little white wood structure, perhaps a store in another life. But it was now called God's Little Acre Missionary Baptist Tabernacle, and it beckoned to her. She aimed that afternoon to check it out. She got as far as the boundary to Maria's property.

Hey Missus. And Maria waved. Come have some nice biscotti. Fresh from oven.

Biscotti? Ole Granny didn't have the foggiest notion of what biscotti was. She really didn't even understand what the lady was saying. She just stood still and stared at her. She didn't know what to make of Northern white people; she was still too fresh from the South. So she just stood there, not wanting to be rude but not knowing what to do.

Maria coaxed her. Come, come. Is OK. Come. I'm Maria. Come Missus.

And Granny climbed the wide stairs to Maria's porch by holding on to the old-fashioned metal handrail. It was sturdy; Maria's son had recently re-anchored it. How do, Maria, My name is Ola Mae Hendrik. Please to meet you.

I'm Maria Vitale. Nice to meet you, too, Missus Hendri, sit. I go get de biscotti. Sit. And Granny sat on Maria's glider with the big yellow flowered cushions. In no time at all Maria reappeared with a plate of biscottis and sweet iced tea. Granny was in heaven. You make sweet tea, too? Where I come from that's about all we drink. Thank you, Maria. And the two hit it off right then and there with Granny talking about Athens and the South and Maria talking about Sardinia and the mountains. Not to say that the conversation moved smoothly; neither quite understood the other because of their heavy accents. But converse they did with looks, gestures, and the warmth of a budding, genuine friendship.

About three biscottis each into the conversation, Granny asked, What you put in these biswhatties?

Maria laughed. Biscottis. I put de anise, you know like the black long candy the kids eat.

Oh I got cha, like licorice. That's what this tastes like. I knew it was tasting familiar. Just then Eva from across the street joined them. Already she and Maria were friends, and after introductions, the three locked in as if they had known each other all their lives.

Maria, whose English was often still a little rough around the edges, called Eva, Missus Lucky because she had difficulty with Lukow. She called Ola Mae, Missus Hendri.

Thus began their near daily meetings at Maria's. Though she was still healthy enough to shuffle around the house and occasionally venture to someone's place, it was more difficult for her to move around than the others. So Ola Mae and Eva would most often gather at Maria's place. They would recount their stories over weak hot tea in the winter, fixed according to Eva's specifications with barely a hint of golden brown; she said it was healthier that way. In summer they drank sweet tea fixed by Granny herself, plenty of sugar, to give them a jolt, she claimed. There's an amazing amount of wisdom that passed from southern to northern Europe and then over to Athens, Georgia, where all of it combined to enrich the lore and culture of the block.

Not long after the first encounter with Maria and Eva, Granny began attending God's Little Acre Missionary Baptist Tabernacle. The name was longer than the building was wide, leaving the deacons to decide on breaking the name into rows like this with "tabernacle" split across the door.

GOD'S LITTLE ACRE

MISSIONARY BAPTIST

TABER   NACLE

The church had to go that way with the signage in order to leave room to advertise the hours of service on one of the only two windows. On the other, the deacons thought it prudent to display the pastor's favorite inspirational slogan: IF YOU STAND BY THE LORD, HE WILL STAND BY YOU.

God's Little Acre's humbleness attracted Ola Mae, in addition to its proximity. She found herself praying along with the others in its tiny interior almost every Sunday. She could never convince her daughter or son-in-law to go with her, but now and again the five-year-old granddaughter would go in order to wear the flouncy dresses her grandmother bought her.

One day after several years attending the church, the pastor and deacons and elders and church mothers determined that she should be that year's Mother's Day feature, which would mean that she would now have her own chair right in front of the pastor in the corner of the second row. She would be escorted henceforward by an usher to her special seat, and from then on she would never have to rise for another church member. The usher would march them around wherever to avoid that. On her day the church gave Ola Mae flowers and a special crown, special prayers, and a citation that noted her special communication with the Lord Savior, through which she connected the entire neighborhood. And almost the entire block attended the presentation that Mother's Day at the little church on its northernmost corner, including Eva and Maria, who claimed that she had gone into the church once or twice when little girls on the block received baptism. Dat was a long time, long time ago. Beyond God's Little Acre, some of the first stages of what would later be called ruination were beginning to develop, one or two empty former homes in various stages of decline. But on that block at that period of time, some of the symptoms of urban decline had not yet hit. No drug dealers, no unexplained fires, no vagrant inhabitants. None of that yet because of the informal forces of protection such as the horseman and his sons and the beefy workers, the old timers who peeped out of windows at every strange movement on the block. And, of course, Granny's special communication with the Lord.

About an hour before the hot dogs, the neighborhood was humming, knee-deep in dirt and anticipation. Happy by now with the smell of the grill and the griller's sounds as it became clearer to all that work would be coming to a good, relaxing end. The block, long known for its dazzling purple irises and tulips, had color already. Spring was already showy; they were prepping for summer and beyond. Granny, Eva, and Maria had long lost interest in orchestrating the proceedings; they were engaged in their usual round of stories, memories from past days, mini-educationals on their respective cultures by the time Eva looked up in the middle of a laugh and saw him. The other two could tell something was wrong by the way Eva's lips froze, eyebrows knitted together. Her face slowly went from a pale rose to gray. She looked horrible and shocking because, believe it or not, all three of these women were gorgeous for their age. Especially Eva, who was the thinnest and the most put together in terms of dress and makeup. She was the youngest by a couple of years and still was out and about, driving herself to and from her restaurant job, and had a gentleman friend who took her to dinner and a show now and again and visited her home. And who could be seen leaving early, early in the morning from time to time. So when Maria and Granny saw Eva's brows and frozen smile and gray coloring, they swiveled their heads around and knitted their eyebrows, as well. Eva expelled a soft shhhhhh and all lowered their eyes as if nothing was happening, but they peeked as well as they could to track the movements of the tallest man any of them had ever seen. Granny whispered that he must be at least seven feet tall, but they were sitting in rather low chairs, which gave them a strange point of view. From where they sat his head was small and his body large and pear-shaped. His face was pasty and featureless, his chest round and soft looking; his mid-section was the shape of a truck tire and his lower section flat and wide. He almost looked like the Michelin Man, except that nothing about him was cuddly. The three women looked over and around at each other while fighting to keep their heads down. Occasionally, one or the other would hazard a glance at him, and for the first five minutes or so he didn't see them. He may not have seen anyone's face because the rest of the neighborhood was bent over digging and planting, with the exception of the horseman, who gave the strange man one puzzled look then turned to assist his son with hauling a wheelbarrow full of manure to a spot north of where the ladies were sitting. The man's presence may not have even registered with him or anyone else in the neighborhood, except the three women. The man entered the block from the south, the side farthest from God's Little Acre, which made Granny immediately suspect that he was related to the devil. They watched him a few more minutes as he assessed the area and then began walking from address to address, crisscrossing the street as he moved north before heading south again past the ladies.

His shirt was white, blinding white, so white that it reminded all three women of the bluing they used for decades to get their Monday wash whites just that brilliant. His tie was a conventional striped blue and white or gray and white or blue and gray; they couldn't quite tell. His pants were a Robert Hall cut and dark gray, almost black. Eva immediately associated him with death. He's come for one of us, she whispered. Maria, the oldest of the three, sat still, only allowing her right hand to grab the left for comfort and control. Granny noticed and reached over for her hand. Eva took the other one. So, the three sat in quiet speculation about the purpose of this man on the block while he continued to dart from one spot to another, as if looking for the correct address. Maybe he's lost, said Granny. Maybe he's on the wrong block and doesn't realize it. But something told her to not holler out to offer him assistance.

Her voice hoarse and weak, Maria said, Yes, I think he is here on death business.

Eva, sorry that she had brought up death, said, No, no. Not that, some other business.

Granny agreed, No, not death. Death don't carry a notebook like that man carryin. Which is what the man had clasped just at the top of his paunch, a black notebook. He's here for some kind of legal business, added Granny. Maybe he's a bill collector.

Maria brightened at that possibility. Maybe he come to sell insurance. My husband buy insurance from a man like that years ago. He come to the house. Only he was nice and friendly. This one doesn't smile.

Eva, glad to escape from death, latched onto insurance. Yes, he looks like he sells insurance.

Granny shook her head. Naw, insurance men have briefcases cause they have lots of paperwork for you to look at. He ain't no insurance man. He's up to something else.

The three continued to follow his progress. Once when Granny was stealing a peek at him, he looked directly at her, which made her shiver. She swiftly focused her eyes past him as if she had never been watching him in the first place. You know how you can stare at someone and then stare through them when you're caught in the act? Well, that was a technique Granny had developed back home in Athens as a way to track the maneuverings of whites without getting caught. This man gave her a look as if she could be the one he was after, then moved off to the southernmost end of the block were he frantically peered east around the corner, turned his body to gaze north up the street, then looked west, then north again.

No one besides the three women paid him any attention, and he asked no one for help. He said nothing.

Granny, one of God's Little Acre Missionary Tabernacle's Church Mothers, squeezed the fingers of her two companions and whispered, We need to pray. They closed their eyes and held their heads down while Granny muttered incantations to the Lord, recalling his almighty goodness and strength and love for his people. She begged him to lift her block into his lap of mercy and uttered the names of each and every person living there to commend them to his mercy in forgiving whatever wrongdoings they may have committed. Lord, know that they will pay their bills because these are a hardworking and honest people.

With eyes closed and Granny's droning, they fell into a reverie. Lord, know that they will not fornicate outside with outside women or men, know that they will love and honor their kin, know that they will forever live in the glory of your word, my sweet Lord, they will praise your name and treasure the life you give them and not tempt death . . . and on and on she went until noon struck and the neighborhood began to file into the grill master's yard for hot dogs, and the marigolds sought to stretch their roots into the manure-laden soil, and the rose leaves fluttered in the gentle air and the first buds of peony drank in the spring warmth. And the irises listened.

Lord stand by us in this our most hour of need. Stand by us, Lord, even if the moon falls from the sky and the sun refuses to rise. Stand by us. At this, the three again squeezed tight their hands. Maria was trying to recall her husband, but it had been so long. She could remember her son, though. He was as big as the man they had seen but handsome and better shaped and friendly warm, full of anise.

Granny was just trying to pray through this moment that none of them understood, but the man had brought strange vibrations with him that each of the women realized were harmful and bode ill.

Eva didn't have the faith or anise of the other two; she had only them at this point. She was trying to figure out how she had got from over there to here, to this moment. She, too, had trouble remembering things, especially the face of her husband. They were still married as far as she knew. Her daughters wrote her now and again, and sometimes she received a call from them. She could never figure out how their father was able to pull them from her, except that maybe it wasn't him but his country. Maybe they never cared for here. She did. Was that the major difference between them? She was saving, hoping for the day when she would have enough money to visit her daughters. You would think they would send for her. But not yet.

So when Granny and Maria squeezed her hands, they gave her the strength to refocus and to wonder, as she had over the years, how long it would be until things would change for her. Indeed, how long until . . . At that thought, she turned full to Granny and Maria, and the three smiled at each other in a way you could only smile, crooked but firm, like when you are in the full knowledge of what life can give.

Just then the horseman and his sons came over to escort the ladies to the food; the strange man had disappeared.

Five Workers Report on How the Deal Really Went Down

I.

smooth talking rich man
all you got was my body
peace now owns my soul

Wow wee—for seven in the morning, the lights were bright like an RKO studio filming *It's a Wonderful Life* as people began milling around the entrance to the Building D auditorium. We came from all over the site, assembly and metal fabrication, grounds and housekeeping. Some of us looked older than Jimmy Stewart would look right now if he were still alive. We tripped over the closed-circuit TV cables yet to be taped down. We bumped into the public relations contractors who ran around like decapitated chickens trying to get the show ready for the eight o'clock formal rollout of the most historic exit plan the company had ever offered to its employees. The old wheezy benefit rep, stationed at the entrance to the auditorium, greeted each of us with a handshake and a pat on the back, inviting all to grab a donut or bagel. They're diet, he proclaimed. Then he motioned for us to grab the printed handout of the Strategic Action Plan.

Crumbs free falling from my jibs, I sidled up to the rep. You studied the Plan yet?

Yeah, I've been to a couple of meetings on it. It don't look too bad. What else we gonna do? It's their world.

You goin?

I don't know. I still gotta see how the details shake out. I gotta see where the devil is hidin between the lines. It's one thing on paper, something else when things get rollin in the real world.

After sixteen years on the floor as a committeeman and almost ten as a benefit rep, he knew the devil was always somewhere lurking in agreements with the company. He was right there a few months ago peeping from around a corner in that very same Building D when the devil visited the white-collar workers. He told us how it happened—scared the stew out of us. Security forces escorted a slew of salary folks out of company buildings all over the nation on what was called Black Thursday. Oh yes, there had been a variety of packages presented to hourly and salary workers over the past long years of decline and uncertainty in the auto industry, but nothing like that—security forces moving against the white collars and now a Hollywood invitation for all the blue collars to hit the road. The whole world was upside down, even for the asthmatic benefit rep and other union committee folks who crept anxiously around the edges of the auditorium, greeting the membership. They were all in the same boat—union reps, sweepers, production workers, tradespeople, and grounds crews—trying desperately to parse out the management offer, the Strategic Action Plan—or SAP as folks were already calling it—that would affect the rest of their lives.

The auditorium was so transformed that morning you could easily forget you were in a place for auto production, where steel parts and flesh interacted. The maze of black velvet curtains confused even longtime workers as they wended their way past glitzy company logos looming high in the darkened auditorium where all the seats faced the bright stage lights.

Man I feel like a damn deer in a headlight, said one sweeper with a donut balanced precariously on his Styrofoam coffee cup and the SAP handout under his arm. He squeezed next to a coworker from his department. I ain't even seen no security guards.

I told him, They're hiding here somewhere. Mark my words. If they could use them against salary, where do you think we stand?

So the conversations went as we, unusually wide-eyed for that hour of the morning, found seats in the auditorium that in previous times had been the venue for many all-employee meetings. In those days, salary and hourly sat side by side listening to the muckety-mucks tout company progress in sales or quality or to announce managerial realignments that would certainly lead to improvements. It was also the site of the annual Christmas party.

But this all-employee meeting was definitely different. It wasn't about sales or quality or managerial moves; it wasn't a party. This meeting was about the company asking each and every one of its hourly workers, all of us, whether we had five years or fifty, to consider leaving its employ, retiring early, or completely severing his or her relationship with the company. Some strategic plan. This was a forced march out into the wilderness of pension checks or one-time severance payments. Ready or not, there you go. This wasn't even an all-employee session—only the hourly sat on the audience side of the stage while all the managers, from line supervisors to the top guy, crowded on the stage in respectful silence as the program opened with a video presentation of the national anthem and the pledge to the flag. Then a cadre of top-level managers with white shirts, somber ties, and dark suits remained as the rest filed off the stage and positioned themselves along the walls on either side of the hall. Not a one of them smiled or acknowledged us. We began shifting noisily in the seats.

One of my buddies, an electrician sitting in front of me, leaned over to his work partner, What kind of shit is this?

Meanwhile the local union leadership, each with a cell phone visible, huddled to the right of the stage on the main floor behind a bare rectangular table. None of them were smiling either. Why should they? It was management's presentation, but they knew they would suffer the fallout once the song-and-dance routine ended. They would be the ones to listen to our fears while we made decisions to go or stay. They would be the ones to process the paperwork for those who decided to go or unscramble the workload for those who stayed. Either way, they would be holding a lot of hands and drying a lot of eyes and picking up a lot of pieces of blue-collar hearts within the next months.

Some manager with a tight smile sauntered up to the podium as if he were getting ready to announce the winners of a fifty-fifty raffle. Well, ladies and gentlemen, thank you for taking the time out from your busy day to come to this very important meeting.

And he rattled on and on about this historic moment, what it would mean for the growth of the company. On and on and on and on he went about the momentous opportunity and our strategic role in the future of the company and then what that means for the nation. Unreal.

Finally, someone in the audience yelled, Cut the crap; give us the plan. The manager clammed up fast and looked around the stage to the others, fixing his eyes on the top manager, Mr. Big Stuff, who then nodded yes. So the rambling manager began an introduction of Mr. Stuff, including all the positions in the company he had occupied—here and there, in Mexico, in China, in Europe. And now he is the new head of Labor Relations for American Operations.

We had all heard this shit before whenever they introduced a Mr. or Ms. Big Stuff, as if they were the salvation of the company. There was a time we bought into all of that, honestly thinking that maybe this Mr. or Ms. Biggie could be the right stuff for the business. We would actually analyze their first one hundred days, how they walked, if they acted snooty or regular, were they micromanaging or giving us free reign to do our jobs.

According to the rambler, Mr. Stuff was the seventh son of the seventh son and very close to saving the world. By this stage of the game, we knew the bullshit. If this guy was so great, why in the hell was the company trying to get rid of us? Was he so great that he and the rambler could make cars by themselves? Someone leaned over to me and said, They must think we're fools.

Naw, man, they think we're SAPs. Got it?

Then the real spiel began. We listened wide-eyed as the message unfolded. In the Strategic Action Plan there was, indeed, something for everyone, absolutely everyone. If you had five years, you could get a small lump sum and a fond adieu as you signed off on all health and any other benefits. The more years you had, the larger the lump sum and the riskier it would be to sign off. Those of us with thirty or more years could take the lump sum and sign off or take regular retirement and get another kind of lump sum. Man it was confusing. Soon the whole auditorium sounded like crickets at sundown as each began turning to the other for clarification.

Did he say that? He couldn't have said that.

I don't know, man. Sounds crazy to me.

Hands shot up. Mr. Big Stuff began fielding questions. Yes, you can take the early out option and still get your pension. You have to have twenty-eight years. Yes, you can still get your health benefits. If you have fifteen years, you can get a lump sum, start a business. Well, no you wouldn't have health care. This plan is ideal for someone with a spouse who has health care. Say, if your spouse works for us, then one of you can take the buyout and the other a regular retirement and both can have health care on the one's regular retirement. You'd be sitting pretty then. No, you don't have to take a buyout if you have thirty or more years.

Then someone asked the huddle of union reps what they thought of the plan. That's when the shit jumped off. Right away the head bargainer brought up that jobs were leaving the site like forty going north. This plan may save the company, he said, but it sure ain't saving our folks.

Yeah, said another, you guys are just flat-out liars; you don't know how to manage the business.

The rambler got real hot. He was trying his best to defend the company. Mr. Stuff stepped back a bit from the mic and adjusted his tie and suit jacket. He was trying to stay cool and above the fray while the rambler and the reps continued to argue about the relative merits of the Strategic Action Plan. That didn't last long; soon the Stuff was just as loud as the rest. Hey, look, the main thing to remember is that you have options. You really have options here.

Good grief, you would have thought they had all that shit smoothed out ahead of time, but then what happens at the upper levels of the union and management doesn't always trickle down to local level, where the real dirty work happens. It was a riot up there on the stage, and on the floor every last one of those union reps was on a cell phone calling someone about something. They forgot all about us.

Hey, can I ask a question? My buddy next to me jumped up. You could hardly hear him over the arguing. Hey, hey, he yelled out.

The whole crew on the stage and the reps on the floor shut up tighter than a drum and turned toward the questioner.

So what if I don't want to go til the end of the year and what happens to the lump sum and my taxes?

At that the big Kahuna readjusted himself and revealed that it was the company's intention to roll out the offers in waves in order to avoid a mass exodus. That way we can maintain continuity and guard the health of the business.

Right away you could hear folks jabbering about which spike of the wave they wanted to ride. No use reporting the graphics of how some demonstrated riding the wave. Suffice it to say some wanted early outs; some wanted to wait until the last day of the year.

The CEO guy and the union reps were working together by this time to quiet folks down so that any one of them could attempt to answer the second part of the man's question.

Too late. That same guy with the question turned to the audience and began waving his arm side to side like they do at the baseball games. OK everybody—see if you can catch this wave.

I couldn't believe it. Even I stood up and was moving my right hand back and forth, my eyes wetting up, thinking about my wife at home. We don't have kids, but she's been ill for so long. And I know for a fact my buddy doing the waving has two kids in college and a third with a major health problem. We weren't ready to go.

The whole auditorium moved hands and bodies back and forth, everyone, that is, except those on the stage and the union reps. All in front froze as all of us silently waved back and forth, back and forth. We were cutting through that stale auditorium air without one word, without one sound.

Finally, a woman jumped up and stood on her seat so she could be seen. She surveyed the waving masses and mumbled to herself. Then she yelled out at the top of her voice, What is going on here? What's with these waves; this ain't no Prince concert; this ain't no baseball game. Now tell me where do I sign up? I'm ready to wave bye-bye now.

II.

s*istah mama lives*
a*s you could never believe*
p*ossibility*

The walk back to my job from the auditorium was like walking back through time to ten years ago when they had a similar meeting way cross town from here to announce that my old plant was closing. After that meeting folks were huddled like schoolyard children in corners everywhere just like this time, but back then they were crying and praying they could make the cut. Ten years ago the company wasn't offering money for us to get out of its sight. The message was, in so many words, you better have enough seniority to go to another plant or get ready to call that unemployment number.

Naw, this time these folks weren't crying after the meeting, but they were still in little knots of three and four in every little hole you could imagine trying to figure out what the man had just told us. They even had papers and calculators out adding and re-adding the figures. Some of them were still by the auditorium arguing with the union people. What for? It ain't the union reps' world. Lawd Almighty, everyone was so lively, almost happy like they had a new purpose in life. Stragglers like me could hardly pass by without someone shouting, You goin? Lawd today, what they need to know for? As if what I have to say could help them with their figurations and calculations and what not.

No there wasn't one soul crying. Downtown, ten years back, almost everyone was crying, whether they did it out in the open or not. I wasn't any different; I was crying, too. But my tears dried up when I found out I would be one of the fortunate ones who didn't have to draw unemployment. Then my tears started up again just seeing things go down so. And they dried up trying to figure out how to make it in a new place with new people. My eyes were dry but my stomach was in knots throughout the first year here. Then you really settle in because at least you're drawing a weekly check. And now this mess. Mess or not, whatever they want to call this here plan, I still need the weekly check. And this time I have a choice.

So I'm just waddling down the hall that connects the auditorium building to my place of work and this one and that one was yelling out to me, Big Mama, what about you? You goin? I smiled and shrugged my shoulders and acted as if I was contemplating things. You can't let folks peep your hole card, but I knew full well, Big Mama wasn't goin nowhere. Weary as I am. Lawd knows some days my arthritis hardly lets me get out of bed and my legs swell up so from my heart condition, but Big Mama can't go, not just yet.

Yes, Lawd, what a crazy day, just like downtown ten years ago; the morning was already shot. Nobody was in any hurry to get back to the job because no one expected any work from us. I guess that was our so-called perk, giving us time to absorb the official offering. Although weeks ago we all knew it was in the works. We were getting little bits and pieces all along, more from the newspapers than anywhere else. Then we'd have to pry information from the committee people. The foremen didn't know a thing. They were like scared chickens, praying they wouldn't be next. We all knew high management wasn't through getting rid of low-level management. You could sense it in the supervisors' attitudes toward us. They were getting real intimate with their insecurity and began treating us more gently than I ever remembered in my thirty-five years working for this company. That was the nicest I'd ever seen some of them bastards. But as far as I was concerned, it was too late for them to even think of treating me human. I know the Lawd says forgive and forget, but I wasn't quite there yet. Jesus, help me.

Out of nowhere someone hugs me by the waist and gives me a big kiss on the cheek.

Who is that? Oh Lawd, gal, you ain't through jumpin up with your excitement? I'm so happy for you.

Big Mama, I already made my appointment to see the benefit rep. I'm getting out of here. Yes I am. I've put my time in and I'm gone. Enough is enough.

And she kept hugging my waist and practically pushing me down the hall and yelling out to everybody, I'm goin. Matter of fact, color me gone now. Nobody needed to ask her intentions; she almost broke up the meeting when she jumped up and asked for her papers. One thing we could all say about her, she never said a peep about anything. She just went along with everything the man told her to do. She was a good and quiet worker. So when she jumped up in the auditorium, hallelujah, it was like Saturday night prayer meeting. I believe that girl got saved.

So what about you, Big Mama? You goin?

Lawd, here we go again, but I had to be truthful with her because she didn't have any backdoor intentions. Bless her heart, she just wanted to know what was happening with Big Mama.

Naw, baby, I told her, Big Mama ain't goin nowhere. I been studyin and studyin every scrap of information I've been able to get my hands on. I already talked to the benefit man. Naw, Big Mama can't go, baby, too much goin on at the home front.

Now she stopped the both of us right there in the middle of everything and commenced to lookin at me as if I was crazy. So I had to tell her, That last one, you know how it's been with him. I got to help my baby through this terrible time. The Lawd done put a trial before him; I got to help him get through it.

Big Mama, the Lord helps those who help themselves. You've raised four children. That boy is in his thirties. It's your time in life now. Take the money and run to the Bahamas, Jamaica, Cancun, somewhere. Take a cruise, Big Mama. Get you a new wardrobe. Get you a man.

Now that left us both laughing like hyenas. Everybody stopped talkin to look. So I had to tell them, You all go on with your calculatin and figuratin and leave Big Mama and Miss Free-at-last be. We got things to discuss, too.

They all went back to their conversations, but my girl just wouldn't let it go with me. Big Mama, promise me you'll take another look before the deadline. Call your financial advisor and let him help you work out the figures.

I've been talking to my financial advisor, baby. I've been prayin and prayin on it; I even talked to my pastor. Lawd knows, it ain't time, yet. I just got to get rid of one more. One more.

Big Mama, don't die in this place.

Naw, baby, Big Mama ain't dying nowhere near here.

That's what I told her, but deep down inside, I wonder. Yes, Lawd, I truly wonder.

III.

s*erious love now*

a*llows me constellations*

p*ast many black holes*

Talk about being lost in a fog. I'm not sure I heard a word anyone said, except for when that woman jumped up. Truth is I spent the entire time eating donuts and rehashing my life AGAIN because I already knew weeks ago when this whole Strategic Action Plan came up that I wasn't going to be able to go anywhere.

Have you ever arrived at the realization that your life has gone ahead of you in a direction and a distance you never figured? And that everything has gotten beyond your control without you even knowing, without your consent? A little of this and that has climbed into your world and fenced you in? No, ambushed you, locked you in the Jaws of Life. Or is it death? Now here you are, flopping like a fish on a hook or a mouse in a trap baited with stale peanut butter.

My buddy leaned over to me after the meeting and asked, Hey man, you going?

Naw, I'm too young.

That's the time to go. Don't wait until you're old and rickety like me.

Don't worry; I'll be out in a couple of years, I told him.

You know as well as I do that two years won't make that much difference in your finances. If we ain't made it by now, we won't make it in two years—unless we hit the lottery. You know what I mean? Take what they're giving you now and hit the road, Jack. You still got a lot of life ahead of you. You could start a business or something.

Can't, man; you know I got a young wife.

She can help with whatever business you start.

Well, you know how women are.

Oh-oh, I bet she wants a baby.

Well, you know you can't deny them. He he.

I can't tell him the truth. My wife doesn't want to get pregnant. I even suggested we adopt, but she doesn't want to do that. Here I am with a beautiful wife, no kids and debts up the ass. How did this happen?

My buddy walked with me back to the job. We've worked side by side ever since I arrived at this facility so I know he has his finances straight. He had numbers crunched even before we found out about SAP. He's got the seniority, and he and his wife have been working as a team over the years to prepare for retirement. He has it all figured out. So now that we've had the official rollout of the program I ask him, more out of formality than anything else, You goin?

Hell yeah I'm goin. I was ready anyway. This is just icing on the cake.

Goddamn, how did this happen to me? This is the third time I've been in a buyout situation in this company, and I still can't take advantage of it. The first time was downtown. I could have qualified for something, but the company refused to call it a plant closing so nobody got anything except the boot to a new location or to the streets. So I lost out. I shouldn't say I lost out; at least I was relocated. But I was young enough then. I really could have started a whole new career if the company had offered a package. That could have been a golden opportunity. The second time was here, a few years ago. The company offered buyouts, but the way they set that deal up, I didn't have seniority or age. And now I'm on my third strike. And I'm out. What kind of a loser am I? I know something like this ain't coming my way again.

We're almost at our workstation now. Someone hollers out, You gonna be a SAP and stay or you gonna take the money and be a gone SAP?

I'm a staying SAP. Someone has to do the work. Someone has to be loyal to the company.

That gets a big laugh out of everyone. Yes, I was single and free as a bird. Then I got the damn bug because of my buddy. Because of him and his damn good marriage. They had me over a few times for dinner and I saw how great he and his wife got along. Their kids are grown, real nice kids, too, and now my buddy has grandkids. What a wonderful life. They spend their summers up north and spend the fall preparing for the Christmas season. It's always a big deal in his household.

Well, I thought I could do the same thing, you know. So what if my first marriage failed. I figured I was young enough to try again. After all these lonely years fumbling along like a fool, building my house, fixing cars on the side to make extra money, paying off my time-share, cutting corners here and there, building up my 401K, hardly even dating, saving money, and for what? The nights get really lonely with only a cat to snuggle up to. As I got closer to getting out, I realized I didn't feel like spending my retirement traveling by myself. So what did I do? At fifty-two years of age I decide to play the online dating game. No shit. I signed up for one of those internet dating services. At first, my buddy thought I was nuts, until he saw how busy I was dating these really nice-looking women and all of them with some kind of talent or the other. I even dated a lawyer once.

I'd come in Monday mornings after one of my dates, and we'd discuss the pros and cons—how she talked about her past relationships, how she acted, was she too greedy at dinner. Did she drink too much? What were her hobbies? After a couple of years and one relationship that looked like it was going to fly but ended up biting the dust, I hit the jackpot with my current wife. Oh yes, I married the most beautiful girl in the world. Man, she was gorgeous. I saw her picture staring back at me from my computer and I almost flipped. I read her comments in her profile and she was sounding sassy—my kind of gal. I had waited a long time for her to enter my world.

Yeah, when I started bringing her around, even my buddy looked a little a jealous. His wife was nice as she could be toward her, but I could tell she was looking at how young and pretty my gal was. She still is gorgeous to look at, but she won't do a damn thing. Once we got married, she quit the little job she had. I told my buddy I wanted her to quit so she could rest up for childbearing. I was too ashamed to tell him the truth. How are we going to have babies if she won't have sex? That fell apart within the first year of marriage. One thing I can say, though, she keeps a nice house and she loves cats.

My buddy and I got back to the job and began organizing to start the press. I was beginning to wonder if anyone could say anything besides, You goin? Could people please talk about the weather, anything but this damn plan?

So I turned to my buddy, who's about fifty pounds heavier than I. Hey, man, can I ask you a favor?

Shoot.

Is there any way you could order some work pants and shirts before you go? He looked at me like I was nuts. I mean in my size? For me. It's not like you'll be needing them.

IV.

so I feel angry
as if I ain't got no right
push me one more time

I was already back at my work area when they all began trooping by me. Big Mama walked by looking the same as ever—not happy, not sad—so I couldn't get a read on her. But I was guessing she wasn't taking the money because even she would be a little happy looking if she was getting out. Don't you think? I mean, except for Big Mama, you could tell right off the bat who was going and who wasn't, even the ones who didn't have a big silly grin on their face like that woman who jumped up in the meeting—man she was all over the place slapping folks on the back, high-fiving, doing little dances up and down the aisle, all the while talking into her Bluetooth, probably to the benefit rep or maybe her financial advisor. Who knows? She was off the hook. Looked like she forgot all about work.

So aside from her obvious self, everyone else going had a modest smile or their bodies had that relaxation look about them. They were shuffling back to their jobs nice and slow, like they didn't give a damn about none of that stuff anymore, like they were already in another world, the real world. You take my friend; he looked happy as I don't know what as he wandered into the auditorium. I was watching him and some of our other coworkers as the meeting kicked off. And I could feel their joy clear across the other side of the room.

But it was just too much for me. I left that meeting early. There was no point in me staying. I could tell the man had folks just where he wanted them, marching out to the streets grinning like clowns with not-so-fat checks in their hands once Uncle Samuel got his big chunk. And then they would have to live on retirement checks and who knows how long that shit would last. I had made up my mind weeks ago that I wasn't goin. These muthafuckas weren't gonna make me go, they weren't gonna buy my ass out to save their rich hides; I wasn't gonna be their SAP. So why should I stay and listen to their bullshit? So I just hung around long enough to get a free cup of coffee and a couple of donuts, and adios, sayonara, and all that good stuff, I was outta there.

My very best friend out here came up to my workstation. He was one of the last to get back to the area; he must have been back there at the auditorium talking to the union folks or whoever about getting out. He came up to me with all teeth showing. So I told him right off the bat, Close your mouth, man, I don't need to see all them teeth. I didn't know you had so much in there. Are they all yours?

Man, hush up, all these teeth is bought and paid for. And I'm a brand-new me, cuz they getting ready to set me free. Ha ha, how do ya like them apples? So you goin, man? You change your mind?

You know I ain't goin.

Why not? You got years to spare, man. Matter of fact, lend me some of yours, cuz I'm goin no matter what. Maybe I can get a dollar or two more with a couple of your years. You got enough.

I ain't got nothin to give nobody right now. Yeah man, I'm stayin here till the cows come home and quit giving milk. I'm gonna be the one to turn off all the lights in the barn, you dig?

Well you are welcome to it, brother, because I'm gone. This is it. I don't think another offer like this will come our way.

The line started up nice and slow. Good thing, because people were sauntering back to the job as if they were going to a summer social. My friend and I were both sweepers, so we weren't tied to the line. We sat over by the picnic table. He commenced right away trying to convince me to go, and I felt obligated to get him to stay.

Look, man, I asked him, have you run down all the figures. You know you ain't prepared to make this move.

I've been runnin down the figures, he said. I can make it. The wife and me have been saving for years for this moment. I've been stashing money away in the 401K like crazy. Between her pension and mine, we got it covered.

And let me ask you something else—ain't your wife at home these days?

Yeah, she retired a couple years ago.

So wait a minute, you want to stay at home with her all day long? Does she even want you at home with her? I know mine doesn't, and I don't want to be with her. That's one of the main reasons I ain't goin.

Man, I never thought about that. Wow, I guess I'll have to get me something to do out of the house to make a little extra money, or volunteer or something. I can't sit at home.

I knew I had him on this point; his wife ain't exactly easy to get along with. If I put the two of them together, I believe she's meaner than mine and mine ain't no Sunday school picnic. Look, man, why look for something to do outside of the house to make extra money when you have something right here to do? It's not like you're working hard.

Naw, man, I'm tired of punching clocks.

Are you sure about the pension lasting? Every day you read the papers somebody's pension is folding up and the workers ain't got nothin. I knew I had him on this one. But he came right back at me.

So wait a minute, man, what makes you think if you stay here forever there'll be a pension for you?

He had me there, but not by much. Listen, man, if all of us old-timers leave, who's going to put into the pension fund? The new young ones they want to replace you with will make half what you make now? How much are they going to contribute to your retirement? You know that's what they want to do? Replace you with someone making much less and getting less insurance benefits. You know that, don't you? Wait a minute, man, how am I going to stop that? I don't want to work here until I'm ready to die. How many fellas you know died a day or two after retiring? I want to enjoy a couple of pension checks before I go.

He almost had me on that one.

Matter of fact, when I retire, I believe I'm going to do some work to get folks elected who care about protecting our pensions. I'll have the time to volunteer to help make this democracy work for us.

Ah man, you've gone all the way crazy now. You never know what elected officials will do. They're all politicians. Democracy my ass. I'm stayin here to make every last bit of this good money I can and go when I get ready and only when I get ready.

V.

*soldiering ain't easy
after one war another
puts bullets in hearts*

Down here in this section of the line we are lucky because not only are we close to the exit by the yard and picnic table, we are close to the cafeteria. So every morning before the line starts I rush up to the counter and order two egg sandwiches to eat when the line starts up. I've been doing that ever since I've been working for the company, even when my jobs were up the line. Nothing in the world tastes as good as those sandwiches as the line jerks forward. When I'm not at work, I don't eat them. They don't taste the same. But you better believe I've eaten bookoo egg sandwiches right here on this line.

I had just come back from the auditorium after swinging through the cafeteria for my two sandwiches, scrambled eggs on wheat toast and butter, when I got hit with their questions. They hollered out to me from the yard.

Hey, amigo, what's shakin? So you figured out what you goin to do?

A group of them sat at the picnic table, and they began bombarding me with questions about the package we were being offered. Not one of them had bothered to go to the meeting, but now they want to ask me bookoo information about the deal, and I'm hungry as all get out and don't feel like talking. Still, these young guys don't know any better, so in between bites of my first sandwich, I told them, Well, I figured out what I'm not going to do. After retirement, I'm not going to eat any more of these sandwiches.

So you are going. Congratulations, they said in unison. Then the kid who works directly across from me asked what it felt like to be a short-timer.

I need something to look forward to twenty years from now, he said. He's a real nice fellow, helps me out a lot. So I tell him and the others like it is just as I finish up my first sandwich.

You won't believe this, but I can't sleep at nights. I'm happy to go, but it's also a little bit like death if you know it's approaching and you have the opportunity to think about it.

I don't know what got into me to say all that, maybe the retirement thing, but I kept on going in spite of their blank faces.

I suppose you reach a point where you are impatient to cross over to the other side, whatever that is—whether your energy will float and be happy and helpful on the other side, or if it will be trapped and agonized. In a way, I am realizing that I am closer to death, but aren't we all, every day of our lives, closer to death? And who knows when death will come; it could be tomorrow for anyone at any age.

Everybody fell silent. Someone said, Shit man; that thinking is way down the road from where any of us are at.

That's when I slammed my stick on the table. I've been carrying it with me ever since the plan came out in the newspaper because I knew I was going. So I roll the stick on the table to make a little noise with it. This is what I said to the guys. You see this? It's my short-time stick. They all looked at me as if I was crazy. Any of you ever been to Nam? All of their heads went side to side.

Of course, not, you're all too young. That's when I proceeded to tell them about how we carried short-time sticks in Vietnam when we were getting close to going home. We'd get a branch from a tree and make a stick out of it. Then we would notch it for every day remaining on our tour of duty and walk around the camp as if we were five-star generals. So if one of them sergeants came around wanting us to do something crazy or dangerous, we'd wave that stick at him. As each day passed, bringing us closer to leaving, we'd cut off a notch. By the time we got out of there, we'd get on the plane with a stub. I still have my Nam stub at home. Now I'm working on my retiring stub.

Wow man, that's heavy.

Heavy? You want to know something heavy? I'm going to tell you something really heavy that happened about a month or so before it would have been my turn to make a short-time stick. It was a day just like today, bright and sunny but hot as the dickens. I was on a mission with about four other guys in this field of grass that was taller than any of us. I don't know the real name of it, but it was so tall we called it elephant grass, and the edges of it were sharp like a razor. It was everywhere in Nam where I was.

The day was still as death. Not a bird was flying, not a bug, not a blade of elephant grass moved. Not a breeze anywhere. The only way that grass would move is if one of us did, and we were being real still. So we must have been sitting there for an hour or so, not moving one bit—believe me, if anything prepared me for working in the factory, it was Nam, because you had to develop the patience of Job in order to survive.

So we were sitting in these clumps of grass being real still when all of a sudden the grass moved right in front of me. Out from behind a really tall and wide clump came this VC. Goddamn, talk about pissin in my pants. That was the closest I'd ever been to one of them. So there we were the two of us staring at each other with our guns pointed directly at each other's heads. The VC was just a boy like me. I could tell. And he was the exact same brown as me. If it weren't for the eyes, he could have been my cousin. Even so, I got some family down home in Aguascalientes that look like they're half Chinese. What I'm trying to say is that he must have realized as much as I did that we were two humans with no personal hatred of each other but caught up in somebody else's conflict. We must have stood there for half an hour or so—to tell you the truth it felt like a day—with our weapons trained on each other, each waiting for the first one to fire. I'll never forget the look in that boy's eyes, the fear, the hope that the moment would evaporate like the sweat was evaporating off our faces. We were both so scared. I realized that boy had a family and wanted to live as much as I did. Just then, the boy backed up against the grass, and it began waving so slow and graceful. Believe me, everything happened so fast after that, the panic in his eyes, the grass waving in the sun, and the awful noise of the rifle.

My coworkers didn't say a word. It got kind of uncomfortable at the table, like that day, sunny and still until the grass began waving. I understood at that moment when the VC kid moved that one way or the other I was going to cross over to the other side. In a way I was between la espada y la pared, ¿tú sabes? Or as they say here, between a rock and a hard place. Then like a light went off or something, the kid who works across from me asks, So wait a minute, amigo, tell us what happened. What happened to the VC kid?

What did he want to hear? Details? There was no more to say; I had already said too much. These guys here now knew more than my wife of thirty-two years. So I just stared at my coworker's hairline—not his eyes, definitely not his eyes—trying to figure out what next. What must they think of me now? I just stared at that kid. I think I counted all the red spiked strands of hair sticking out from the front of his scalp by the time my hand grabbed my other egg sandwich for lack of anything better to do at that point. But the damn thing was already cold.

No Puedo Bailar

for Gerardo

Ahi está la pared
Que separa tu vida y la mía
Ahi está la pared
Que no deja que nos acerquemos
      —from the song "La Pared" by Roberto Angleró

When Los Reyes hit the first chord of their signature bolero rítmico, "La Pared," Orquidia jumped to her feet from the rickety folding chair in the basement apartment of an old building on the main drag of southwest Detroit. It was her favorite tune on the CD because it could stand for many different walls of love, for example bittersweet emotional walls might make lovers fear intimacy or their vulnerability in a love relationship. Or the song could stand for all of the misery she and her compañeros in the room with her right then had experienced just trying to come to the city from across many borders and over real walls. Or it could stand for the love of familia—children, spouses, parents, cousins—left behind. Maybe that was the worst part, leaving lovers and loved ones, leaving all those parts of self behind. Or maybe the fear to immerse oneself in new love because of the walls that surround you as you move about the city to work or gather with new friends similarly situated.

The others tapped their feet and snapped their fingers to strengthen tempo, the men in the group waiting to see who was the brave one that evening with enough energy to take on Orquidia.

mía nada más
mía mía nada más

And then their voices joined those of Los Reyes.

¡ah zi!
esa maldita pared

As the song began its crescendo, Carlos lined up shots of tequila on a tall bench that served as a counter for drinks, and Joaquin flipped open caps on bottles of Corona.

Orquidia was winding up her still soft and supple body, all the while recalling one live and magical performance of Los Reyes in the Plaza de Armas in San Luis Potosí, where she had traveled from Oaxaca to spend the summer with her uncle, who was also her padrino. That was all so long ago in another gentler period of time in her life on one special Sunday, in a special plaza on el día de los padres. Orquidia found herself transported to the plaza in San Luis Potosí on a hot night. Many in the city were drawn to Plaza de Armas just to hear Los Reyes, the live band for the evening. They provided music for the danzón performance where those in the crowd craned to see each elegant couple, a don y doña, gliding under the porticos of the town hall. After the danzón they performed their own music, boleros from her grandmother's era, music untainted by yanqui border influence.

Earlier, the plaza was electric with activity. Groups of men and young boys practiced drumming in a military style while buglers blew and marched around as if they, too, were military. Clowns cajoled the crowd into buying jewelry from the various Indian vendors from the mountains or elote mixed with peppers, mayonnaise, and cheese from the many carts that ringed the plaza. The air smelled of sun and corn. Later, hundreds and hundreds of people gathered for the danzón festival in honor of father's day. Some influential people in the city were honored guests. At least a dozen couples all dressed alike—the ladies in beige sequined tops with fringed bottoms and high heels, the men in black tuxedos—performed the formal Cuban-inspired danzón in front of the Government Palace. Orquidia and her cousins squeezed through the crowd to climb on a band shell where they could just barely see the crowd—the dancers were now mere specks—but could sway their bodies back and forth, arms interlocked in time to the music. Then as now her mother's medallion gently shifted from one side of her chest to the other, also in time to the music. She wore the medallion always to keep close the spirit of the mother who died birthing her. Her uncle in San Luis Potosí was her mother's oldest brother and the one closest to Orquidia.

Eberardo gazed longingly at the glittering medallion, watched Orquidia's hips as she dipped and rose to the music as if climbing the wall referenced in the song. He smiled almost lasciviously, well not quite because he was too young for that, but he was rubbing his hands in anticipation of holding hers in dance. Almost every Friday evening anywhere from eight to twelve of them celebrated life with tequila, Corona, and a variety of botanas in Radames's sparsely furnished basement apartment. Always they dressed their Sunday best. Usually the men outnumbered the women, but on this night they were even steven, five of each, not quite partners. Carlos and Joaquin were being faithful to their women back home. But at least two of the men, Eberardo and Radames, had eyes for Orquidia. For sure, Radames yearned for Orquidia's hot body next to his. At work the gringos called him Radman: Hey Radman, bring that box over here, and then take it over there! Radman, yeah, that's a good boy. For her part Orquidia thought Radames had good possibility—plenty man as far as she could tell from the bulge between his legs. And, of course, Eberardo wanted her in the worst way. But as life would have it, Orquidia was most interested in the least attainable of the men there—César. He normally occupied a corner seat in the room, smiling always. He was the one most preoccupied with his former life in Chiapas and what was happening with his children there. Of all in the group he had come from the farthest away, and he was the one least tied to Detroit, in spite of the intense friendship of those who gathered on Fridays. True the brothers Carlos and Joaquin had wives back home, but at least they had each other and their mother's secret tamale recipe—always in the masa, she said, the masa. César had told Orquidia several gatherings ago when she invited him to dance that he could not. No puedo bailar hasta que pueda ver otra vez a mis hijos. He could not or would not dance until he could see his children again. Orquidia, who had no children, sympathized with him anyway, but thought that one little salsa wouldn't hurt the memory of his children and might even revitalize him for the long time ahead before he would be able to see them. Still, although she did not take his rejection of the opportunity to dance with her personally, she accepted César as a personal challenge.

This is how it was every Friday. Carlos, who made and sold tamales as a business with his brother Joaquin, often cooked nopales y huevos at the gatherings to the delight of his compañeros. Joaquin, as usual, assisted. The brothers were from San Luis Potosí, the area where cactus grew as far as the eye could see. All came to wash down the sweat and dirt from their various occupations during the week, although almost all of them still would find themselves on Saturday or even Sunday scrubbing restaurant dishes, stamping out an automobile part or arranging fruits and vegetables in one of the large markets in the city. But Friday evenings were theirs in amistad and mirth. Time to forget everything: immigration problems, familia en la patria, and utilities that may be cut off at any moment. If anyone should want to forget troubles, certainly Orquidia would top the list. She was the one who experienced the toughest crossing, a textbook horror journey north from Oaxaca to Arizona and then across to Detroit. Whoever wants to come to Detroit? Especially after nearly losing a foot in the desert running from the local militia and the dogs. But Detroit was where she landed full of tales about the cabrones in Arizona and laughter in awe that she had survived, so far.

An Arizona dog may have two of her left toes, but no mind; she still had enough of the left foot to assist the right in twirling and stomping her way through the CDs Radames contributed to the Friday gatherings. He had papers of a sort, at least enough documentation to provide him with cover for the odds and ends jobs he hustled reconstructing kitchens and bathrooms, as well as laying tile and other flooring. The papers also protected him for jobs in stamping plants that made parts for larger union-organized auto assembly factories. None of them in the room, no matter what work they did, were in any kind of union. They were their own informal self-help organization. Because of their papers, Joaquin and Carlos were able to get drivers licenses, a major boon because they were often called upon to drive others without any kind of documentation to various appointments. These runs occurred between tamale drop-offs, during which their passengers often arrived to their destination filled with tasty tamales. Radames provided the same service, especially helpful for Orquidia because she didn't know how to drive anyway. ICE, the immigration authorities who prowled the streets of southwest Detroit looking for paperless people, would demand identification of Joaquin, Carlos, their friends, and anyone else looking like them, whether walking or driving, or in their homes, for that matter. So having the ability to drive legally was a little bit helpful for necessary trips that people could not make by bus or taxi. That was the reality of the world out there every minute of every day, except Friday evenings when the crew gathered, each breathing a sigh of relief as their members entered, still free people, for at least that moment.

Esa maldita pared
yo la voy a romper algún día

At this, Orquidia stomped her cowboy-booted right foot to emphasize her intentions to break a wall one day, however it would present itself, wherever, alone if necessary. Another foot stomp and she pulled Eberardo up from the corner, he sheepishly grinned at the opportunity to dance with this woman of desire. He rose, singing with her the chorus:

> *no puedo mirarte*
> *no puedo abrazarte*
> *no puedo besarte*
> *ni sentir de mía*

As he pulled her closer to him, their lips nearly touched, the song ended, and Eberardo held Orquidia a moment longer as the melody lingered in the air and in the hearts of those gathered. All eyes were on the couple, the only ones on the dance floor, established by moving a couch and a few folding chairs closer to the wall.

Carlos called out, Vamos a cenar, indicating that his specialty was ready and that the assorted chips and salsas and frijoles were arranged buffet-style on the tiny counter in the kitchen. Eberardo rushed to fix a plate for Orquidia, indicating his intention by a look and the slightest touch on her elbow, not a direct connection to her bare skin, but just close enough to allow the electricity from his body to cross over to hers through an invisible channel moistened by anticipation and possibility. In this way he escorted her to a seat at the table to wait for her plate. Conchi, a woman who lived with a family in the suburb of Birmingham during the week as the nanny for two little girls, eyed the exchange between Eberardo and Orquidia with glee. He was her cousin and best friend. She knew he suffered from having to leave his novia in Monterrey, and who knew if they would ever be reunited. She linked her arm in his and kissed him gently on the cheek as the two entered the kitchen for food. Radames grunted at Eberardo before entering the kitchen.

By the time everyone had a plate of food in front of them, including César, who normally went last, even after Carlos the chef, it was time for the first toast of the evening. Eberardo, as usual, jumped up with a wish for good health to all, especially to Orquidia, May she keep dancing to bring light and love to our lives. He was a bit of a poet. That initial guzzle of Tequila 1800, washed down by a few sips of Corona, followed by the nopales y huevos, chips, and so on, fueled the first round of discussion—always about work. These weren't typical whiners, complaining of too much work and too little pay. They, indeed, worked too much for way too little money in jobs that were unsafe. César was probably in the worst situation of all of them because he worked for an asbestos removal firm that provided the worst masks and protective equipment of all similar businesses in the area. If it weren't for a guy there, a worker like him, who spoke fluent English and Spanish and who fortunately would speak up for his undocumented compañeros de trabajo, César would never have received decent equipment nor would he have understood the after-work cleansing procedure. Even with those precautions, César wondered if he would return to his homeland, the lush but troubled state of Chiapas, with any lungs left with which to once again hurl laughter at his children and dance in celebration of his return.

Next on the list of topics was always, always a thorough and lively exploration of what they could do to improve their lot. Past discussions included door-to-door approaches to targeted areas in the barrio to talk about migra actions. This they eventually deemed too dangerous; their undocumented selves would be too exposed. For all they knew they could just as easily knock on the door of an immigration officer as that of a sympathizer. The discussion this evening in Radames's basement apartment took an unusual turn perhaps because of a brand-new portrait of la Virgen in the form of a banner Joaquin had been eyeing ever since he arrived. This is what he proposed: We must warn everyone about la migra, Joaquin proclaimed with only the leading edge of tipsy informing his discourse.

¿Como? asked everyone.

La Virgen, he replied, pointing to the banner hanging prominently in the room. This led Orquidia's fingers to caress her medallion of la Virgen de Guadalupe while others scratched their heads in confusion. Joaquin continued explaining the overall intent of his plan for leaving messages from la Virgen to everyone in the barrio.

Radames demanded to know, ¿Y como le vamos a hacer? How are we going to do this?

That discussion would call for at least two more shots of 1800 and another bottle of beer per discussant. Conchi could handle only one shot of tequila, but she was good for at least two beers. Orquidia varied her intake, depending on her engagement with the direction of the discussion. On this night tequila passed her lips almost without touching them, for Joaquin had proposed an adventure that the ten compañeros would debate back and forth with unbelievable passion.

I'll tell you how, said Joaquin, who was now feeling free enough to trot out the English he had to learn in order to sell tamales to the gringo tourists who crossed over from Canada on the Ambassador Bridge. We are going to make up signs in the form of dichos from la Virgen, avisos warning our people about certain things to do if confronted by la migra.

¿Por ejemplo? This was Eberardo's question.

For example, la Virgen dice no abra la puerta. Nunca. Don't open the door for la migra. Never. Joaquin fully showing off his English now. Orquidia and others nodded. They understood.

Laritza, who worked in a Birmingham house next door to Conchi, piped up, A sí, la Virgen dice no firme nada.

Conchi chimed in, No conteste ninguna pregunta. Tell them nothing.

Everyone got the idea. Soon instructions from la Virgen even touched on health issues such as—don't smoke or have unprotected sex. Those were proposed by the two cousins, Adela y Adriana, often lovingly called the "A Team."

The rest of the discussion focused on logistics—how to create the signs, how to post them, both of which could possibly engage several Fridays.

The last of the nopalitos y huevos disappeared along with the first bottle of 1800. The Corona was holding strong on this particular night when emotions peaked at the possibility of a solution. Maybe not a solution but something to do besides commune by themselves and hope alone. La Virgen could be their public show to others, and they would have her power behind them. Maybe they could unite and become something, some people in this land, this crazy city where people who think they are somebodies have no real power anyway. That's what they wanted to say to the world they were in now. You're no better than us. Remember that. But they had each other and la Virgen and a fresh bottle of 1800, a few Coronas, and lots of memory. Orquidia was still going strong. She had placed her medallion inside her shirt for some strange protectionist reason. She had a feeling they had reached a turning point, this grupo, her compañeros in misery and faith and hope, and she needed la Virgen of her mother to be closer to her than ever.

Los Reyes recycled on Radames's one extravagant purchase, a five-CD changer. The selection had now returned to "La Pared." Orquidia perked up immediately and decided that the smiling, silent César needed to get up from his seat and dance. Why not? You can only hold things in for so long. You must let go if only for a moment. Didn't he have a moment for her? Just a moment for her to feel fully herself minus a few toes. He didn't look like a man who cared about toes. The other two did. Maybe. But, of course, she hadn't tried any of them out. But tonight was the night. Maybe. She carried more scars besides her missing toes. César looked more genuine, more forgiving, as if she could take off her blouse and the scars wouldn't offend him. As if he might find a way into her interior past the wounds on the route up her vagina. She wasn't even sure if it could function anymore. There had been more than four-legged dogs after her on the trip through Arizona.

So, sure in the protection and wisdom of la Virgen, she got up again to dance. By this time she was full of 1800 and nopales probably originally from San Luis Potosí. She was feeling the power and support of her tío and padrino and all of the familia over there. Los Reyes hit her favorite section of the song.

mía nada más

mía mía nada más

And Orquidia slapped her hip. The others laughed and clapped.

¡ah zi!

esa maldita pared

She plopped herself in front of César, folds of her long multicolored skirt draped in her right hand, her eyes intent on his. He looked up, startled in a way, but understanding that it was time for him to make some kind of move. You can't get from Chiapas to Vernor Avenue in Detroit, Michigan, in zero to five, no matter what they say. There has to be time for reflection, time to search out truth, time to figure out what is real. Now he was being called upon to place all of that in order and then dance?

Orquidia swayed to the bolero rítmico as she never had, harking memories beyond what she ever experienced personally. How would her mother have done this? That's what she was thinking. But she saw this intense hombre, Don César, the most guapo of them all, guapo in her eyes beholding him sitting there, and she knew she had eight-toed power to get the man up.

And he got up. No he jumped up. Arms, covered as usual in a long-sleeved black shirt, wide like an eagle's wings, eyes closed and one huge smile spreading across his face. Orquidia, in truth, didn't know what César was about to do at that moment. No one in the room knew. The other women grouped close to each other. Radames and Eberardo furrowed their brows in amazement. The brothers shifted to the rear of the room smiling. But they all watched César's outstretched arms, his taut body, his apparent ecstasy, and waited for the performance.

¡ah zi!

esa maldita pared

Making Bakes

For Yvonne

By the sweat of thy brow thou shall eat bread
—From the calypso song "Jean and Dinah," by the Mighty Sparrow

Whole night long I ent sleep from the blasted summer heat. My room was in the front, and I was afraid tief would climb in if I opened the window; plus the little fan was only blowing hot air. Then too I was busy all night making bakes with Mummy. She came to me in a dream for the hundredth time to show me how to make them. Over and over again when she was alive, and even since she died a couple of years ago, Mummy tried her best to show me how to proportion the ingredients and how to knead everything, but I couldn't ever figure out how she could measure the flour by handfuls, the baking powder with her three fingers, the salt with two, and exactly how much Crisco to add. I can't tell you how much time I spend trying to recall if my fingers were the same size as hers and if hers were the same as a teaspoon or tablespoon. But after her death no amount of measuring equipment was equal to her fingers and hands and could help me make the bakes, not even the little tin cup she used. Whether I was making roast bake or fry bake they tended to come out hard or underdone or burn up. So it looked as if the poor old lady was trying again on such a hot night to see if she could make me understand how to make proper bakes. But then again, summer heat never made a difference when she was alive. She would ting up the flour, flough flough and she done. We eating bakes and the whole house filled up with the warmth of them. Since she dead we haven't had decent bakes in this house. Daddy went so far as to question what kind of woman I am who can't make bakes. These people are tough, you know. What kind of thing is that to say to your daughter?

As I reached the entranceway to the kitchen, it must have been six or so in the morning, and there was Daddy by the stove making the morning brew, half Nescafe instant and half evaporated milk just the way Mummy and Daddy always cooked it on the stove in a little tin pan with three spoons of sugar on slow slow fire until the mixture boiled over. This was how the two of them made coffee ever since I know myself. Whoever was up to make the coffee first would stand over the stove stirring the mixture and wait for it to boil over and that disgusting scummy skin to form on top of the coffee. Then and only then did they consider the coffee done. O lorse how these people could make coffee like that and then drink it and spend whole morning long eating bakes and talking a set of ole talk about life back home. Once the coffee boil, the pan would sit lopsided on the stove with the spoon in it until Mummy would wash everything up; these days it's me to wash.

And the spoon is always well covered with the scum. That's the most I can do, wash the pan and the spoon because me ent have patience for boil over and scum forming and all that.

So I leaned against the entranceway rubbing down the skin on my hands and arms as if the bakes dough passed through the dream and stayed on me. I stopped so watching at Daddy in his old pajama bottoms, his merino vest torn under the arms and him stirring and stirring the coffee waiting for it to boil over on this July morning. The back door was open, letting in the same hot air from last night. Morning Daddy. He ent pick my height. Morning nuh Daddy.

He was well intent on that coffee. I could see how he really needed it this morning. He couldn't have slept well himself last night. His room was in the middle of the house right by Miss Lady next door's kitchen. I know no breeze could pass by there, only odors lingering between the two houses from all those heavy, greasy foods she cooks every day, every season. I don't see how those people could eat food so heavy in the summer, a big set of meat and so on.

Anyhow, I found it amusing how Daddy's big belly was leaning over the stove and how he had a little bit of moisture in the creases of his mouth. From where I was standing, his nose didn't even look so wide, and he was looking healthy from the summer sun even though he was only catching it by sitting on the back porch. He looked damn good for his age, you know, big belly and all. And he was looking cool as a cucumber as if we were in January. His hair was already combed, and I could well smell the bay rum.

I remained like that leaning at the entranceway observing the panorama in front of me. I looked over by the sink, and things were clean but shabby looking, you know. The whole kitchen needed a coat of paint. The whole house needed painting, new furniture, rugs, and the whole nine yards. Then all in a sudden my eyes passed over by the windowsill near the stove, and good God all of Mummy's flowers were dead. O lorse, how we let she house plants go like that? How long they dead so? You mean to tell me I come in this kitchen day in and day out, stand by the stove cooking, and I ent see the flowers dead brown, dead dead?

Eh eh, whah happenin? He was so busy with the coffee he can't acknowledge my presence? Ooohoo, hey now, look me here. Finally he turned toward me.

I smelling something stink he said. No good morning, no how de doo. Just he smelling something stink.

Well naturally I sniffed under my arms. True I wasn't looking great; my hair was all ramfled up, my nightgown fitting me like a jimmyswing, and I must have had bags under my eyes, but I wasn't smelling bad, either. So I told him in no uncertain terms, Is your top lip you smelling, Daddy.

I tell you I smelling something stink.

But what on earth was he smelling? I took out the little bit of fowl guts from the chicken I stewed last night. And we didn't have any pileup of garbage in the back since garbage collection was the day before, thanks to Mr. Mayor Young. I think it was the only thing he did for us since he in the Manoogian, improve the garbage collection. Just in case, I cast my eyes by the back door. No, nothing was out there, only Mummy's roses, which fortunately we hadn't managed to kill. I think Mummy was returning to tend her garden because it was still flourishing, by the grace of God because neither Daddy nor I did much out there. Yes, Mummy's roses were all over, and they kept coming back plentiful over the last couple of summers since she died. So I reported this to Daddy. There's nothing here to smell bad, Daddy, only Mummy's beautiful yellow and red roses perfuming the yard.

By this time he was sitting at the table with his cup of coffee waiting for it to cool. Since Mummy died he ent even adjust the amount of coffee to make, so every morning her share was still in the pan after he poured. They both used little teacups to drink the morning coffee. Why not, since for them everything was tea—cocoa tea, coffee tea, and so on?

You not smelling anything?

No no, Daddy, not a thing. Just as I said that I remembered the time years ago when I was thirteen or so and woke up one January morning to find the two of them by the wide-open back door shivering in the cold. They were having a similar conversation about smelling something. What de arse they could smell in cold weather like that was beyond me. But there they were, the two of them with their arms wrapped around each other facing a near blizzard and saying they smelling something stink. What?

I didn't smell anything back then either, but I can ever remember that morning. Mummy was cream colored, fat and short like a little cuddly stuffed toy, and Daddy was tall, brown, and jocular. I took after both of them, tall like him, creamy like her. Oh yes, they well looked like biff and bam. I watched them real good for twenty minutes from the same kitchen entranceway where I am standing now. Then they closed the door and Mummy twisted around and saw me, Eh eh, morning dahlin.

And I said, Whah happenin, Mummy?

And she said. Nothin dahlin. You want bakes?

But before she could begin making the bakes, the two of them shuffled around the kitchen too-tool-bay for sure. Eh eh, I might as well have said I ent hungry. What was wrong with them? I wondered. But they weren't saying a word. Finally, Mummy bent down in the cabinet where she kept a big ten-pound rice can full of flour for the bakes. Then ring, the phone jumped off the hook in the dining room next to the kitchen, shocking all of us. It was too early for Tante to call. Every afternoon, just after lunch Tante would call and Mummy and she would talk talk talk talk talk for nearly an hour on the phone about this, that, and the other ting. This time it wasn't Tante but a crackly voice. I was the one to answer the phone, and all I could hear was a set of static and a voice sounding way far away, Halo, halo. Is cehhhr cehhhr sheee sheee dere? Up to this day, I don't if the voice was man or woman, or the name it was asking for. Daddy Daddy come take this, nuh. I get all nervous because to tell you the truth I sense something was very wrong. One thing I can tell you for sure, it was some island person on the other line talking fast. Me ent able when they talk fast and then the phone going cehhhr cehhhr sheee sheee.

So Daddy take the phone and next ting I know he's saying O lorse and O good God and how and when and all of those words that make Mummy freeze right there by the cabinet with both her hands around the rice pan full a flour pressing it up against the belly. She ent even take off the top. Her face changed radically as if she already knew just what Daddy would report. She could well see something was wrong on the other end of the phone. And so said so done. Daddy said all right all right and could scarcely put the receiver down he was shaking so much. He stop so by the entranceway looking like a frightened little kid because one thing for sure, up to this day Daddy doesn't like commesse of any sort, no confusion. He doesn't like loud noise, arguing or any of that. He definitely doesn't like back chat from me even now. The only person I ever see could talk to Daddy any ole how was Mummy. I see she take a frying pan to him one day and he cowered in the corner by the stove like a frightened cat. I still laugh when I think of that day. But on this morning after the phone call, it was as if he couldn't say a word. Mummy knew right away and simply asked, Who?

He said, Your brother.

John?

You only have one brother, Mummy. He said this with his tongue rolling around on his lips, his eyes wide open, his cheekbones high as they had ever been. Then he paused, not saying a word. Then he resumed. Is John who came to say good-bye for the last this morning. You realize that?

What time he die? Mummy asked.

About then, Daddy replied.

O lorse, now it's only me left, Daddy. She called him Daddy, too. And to boot, he called her Mummy. Believe it or not, they called me Baby.

So Uncle John was my first lesson in spirit coming to announce its death. Actually, he was my first experience with anyone in the family or anyone close to me dying. But I was well chupid in these kind of island tings, their myths and beliefs. So I chimed in, Mummy, spirit can cross water fuh see people? Mummy replied very patiently that a spirit comes to say good-bye wherever its loved ones are. It was only then I see tears in Mummy's eyes that I realized I asked a bad question. I'm sorry Mummy wherever you are now. I didn't mean to make you cry back then.

I found myself lost in all these thoughts about what happened long ago. Back then Daddy was laid off from the shop so there was no money for either of them to go back home for the funeral. Mummy wailed and prayed and wailed and prayed for days. I never see she cry like that before or since. And Daddy looked so defeated, I suppose because he didn't have the money to send her to the funeral. It hurt me to my heart to see them so sad, and I was only thirteen. Ever since then I learned to not think of myself so much; you have to put yuhself in the other person shoes. Poor Mummy.

Just then the pan tipped over on the stove and the spoon rattled. Oh gosh, I nearly piss on myself.

What is dat atall, Daddy said as if he just now wake up.

Oh nothing, nuh, just the pan tipping over. The spoon musta shift.

Aye–ya-yaye, I say to myself, something is going on. But I don't know what. He says he smelling something; I ent smelling nothing unusual in the house. So if some spirit is hanging around here now it ent come to tell me anything. I stop so looking at Daddy to see if I could see some spirit friggin around him.

Ah wha a watch me fuh? He asked.

Nothing, Daddy. I'm wondering what to eat. You hungry?

In truth my mind had gone back to the dream, and all in a sudden I was wondering if she came to tell me more than just how to make de bakes? Wait a minute, wait a minute. Is she the one making the smell trying to tell us something? O lorse. But she already dead? She can't announce that she's dying again.

What an odor, he said again as he inhaled the air with his eyes closed. This is a smell like a dead rat or a human body passing the last gases. You know Mummy used to say that every time there is a smell of garbage but the house is clean, a spirit is passing through on its way to the other world. Your mother could see spirits. I guess they dohn come to me because they know I fraid dem.

Daddy, there is no such thing as spirits.

Don't you say that, nuh. You remember what happened with your Uncle John? Mummy smelled garbage that morning. A little while later she felt something like a leaf brush across her face while she was standing right here at this sink washing the dishes. Then we got the call from home. Her brother dropped down dead. You remember?

No no, Daddy, she was getting ready to make bakes. She was standing in the kitchen with the big rice pan full of flour right here by the table edge.

Don't contradict me, nuh. What the hell you know?

I well shut muh mouth quick. O lorse, what de arse wrong with him? Something is really going on here. We stop so not saying a word for quite a while really, me leaning up against the entrance, he was staring off as if he was in another land. He ent even take a sip of coffee.

Yuh coffee getting cold, nuh. You want me to heat it up?

How long since Mummy dead? he asked.

Two years Daddy.

Ah well, after one time is another.

Yes, Daddy. But we will make it, please God. We will make it. I feel she is still with us helping us along.

You think so?

Oh yes, she comes to me often in dreams.

You ever see she spirit walking about? She ever talk to you?

In the dreams, yes. I never see her any other way. Always in dreams she comes and always with the rice pan full of flour. What else she going to travel with if she coming to make bakes? And I gave a little laugh to relieve the tension because I could well feel his mind was preoccupied with Mummy and death and so on. Ever since Mummy's brother died and then Daddy's sister just a month or so later, the two of them always talked about death as if it was around the corner waiting for them. I spent my teenage years and up to now living with their thoughts of death. It hasn't been easy, you know.

Then he said, She never even comes to my dreams. I don't see her atall atall. I don't even feel her here. You ever feel her presence?

No Daddy. I just see her in dreams.

Well how do you know she's here?

The dreams, Daddy, the dreams. She was a staunch believer in dreams. This is how she communicates with me. You know long after Uncle John died, she told me that for a few nights before he died she dreamt of the two of them as children playing with the dogs in the yard where they grew up. It was quite an elaborate dream. Their mother called them in the house because a storm was coming, but only Mummy went in. Uncle John was hardened, Mummy said, and kept playing outside. He drowned in the storm. That was her dream.

Is so? Oh yes. I forget all about dat. She told me too. So wait a minute, what yuh dream last night when she come by you? You dream something last night?

Oh yes, Daddy. I had a wonderful dream. He was watching every word falling out my mouth while I'm telling him about the dream. I told him how Mummy came to visit me in the dream wearing her old housedress with all those crazy blue and red flowers and the same washout-looking apron. We were right here in this same kitchen,

Daddy. She was at the head of the table where you are sitting right now—Now he's feeling the edge of the table and looking around a little bit—good. Yes, Daddy, and so she was measuring out the flour from the pan with that same little tin cup she kept with the flour.

I had his full attention. You remember how she used to make the circle of flour. She couldn't make it without singing her song. You remember the song? And then a big smile moved across his face.

O ho. So when yuh bounce up on Jean and Dinah, Rosita and Clementina, round the corner posing. Ha ha. Oh yes. O lorse Mummy loved that song. I could well see she dancing and making she bakes and singing.

Yeah, well I bounce up on she singing that same song in de dream last night. You know Mummy had a song for everything. If she was in the garden, she would come with she "Tee Way Tee Way." Invader never surrender and take some kind ole stick and she put the thing up as if she in some stick fight singing, Pui pui, I say tee way, tee way, oh garçon, oh mama mama tee way.

Yes, yes, I can well see she now. O lorse, I does miss Mummy so. He was quiet for a minute or so then he began a slow, low song, like a dirge, Me ent no go see um see um see um; me ent no go see um no mo. I wonder if it's she coming to tell me something. Maybe she's coming for me.

O gosh, don't talk such flitics, nuh. Where you get that song from? She's not coming for you. How you could say something like that, Daddeee? Me ent smelling nothing. Wait a minute. Me ent remember smelling anything stink in the dream either, only the same nice smell of the bakes cooking—we made roast bake last night—and even in the dream, I smelling sausage or bacon something like that to eat with the bakes. But she comes by all the time and never leaves a bad smell. Daddy, you should have seen us making bakes last night. She made that flour into a circle, and put the Crisco, baking powder, and warm milk in the middle, then worked the flour from the edges gradually into the middle with the liquid. All the while she was signing about Jean and Dinah, Rosita and Clementina, round the corner posing, bet your life is something they selling. And she worked that bottom from side to side. O gosh I miss that old lady. Oui foute.

So I'm still leaning at the entranceway—not in the kitchen, you know—but striking a pose like Jean or Dinah or one of them. Then I began to sing and twist around in my jimmyswing nightie and my ramfle-up hair trying to dance like the girls in the song. Daddy ent even pick muh height. He was still sitting in the same spot at the table, looking at the kitchen door and talking talking talking. Now who was he talking to; I ent see nobody. But I heard words like O lorse and good God and when? Is now? I guess so. And then his head lapse, hitting his chest as if he had given up in sadness for some reason, remembering something or wishing Mummy was there, which I could well understand.

So I said, Eh eh, Daddy. Everything will be all right, yuh know. Nuh worry about something stink. Is yuh top lip, Daddy. True nuh. Is the bakes you smelling. Is how I was making bakes whole night long with Mummy that you smelling them this morning. You not smelling anything bad atall. You want bakes? I going to fix them for you now just like Mummy's. You wait and see. Move aside; I coming now for the flour pan. While I was reaching up to see if I could pull my hair back and rearrange myself for the task at hand, I began singing the Jean and Dinah refrain and wining up as if I was in the streets dancing. I was trying to make him feel good. Whoo watch me, nuh, Daddy. Get ready for some bakes. I feel to make real good bakes this morning. Watch me, nuh. Daddy. Daddy. Daddy?

Sometimes You Leap;
Sometimes You Fall

My mother died at the moment I was born, and so for my
whole life there was nothing standing between me and
eternity...

—Jamaica Kincaid, *The Autobiography of My Mother*

One day in spring a question fell
And went straight through me
Do bleeding angels sing when close to tears?

—Terence Trent D'Arby, "If you go before me"

From where she stood at the smoke-yellowed window of the interrogation room on the thirteenth floor of the downtown police precinct,
the gull looked like a big dry leaf or crumpled paper bag swirling on
the ground as if caught in an isolated air disturbance, a mini-tornado,

funneling directly from her tear-filled right eye. She closed that eye, using the left for vision. Then she could see clearly that the gull was pulling on a piece of plastic like a dog tugging at rawhide. It appeared to her aggressive, fearless, absorbed. It fought with the plastic in the middle of the street as cars zoomed north and south of it; only occasionally did its head bob up to scan the area for competing gulls.

With each passing car her left eye automatically shut tight then opened to find the bird still wrestling with the plastic. Way to go, guy. I bet you ain't even afraid of the night.

It was easy to become lost in the gull's motions. What else was there to do after two detectives have had their way with you? After their probing questions? Why this? Why that? Who knows the why of anything? One detective big and black as an ace and bald-headed, the other slight and white. Interchangeable as good guy and bad guy.

OK, OK, Mizzzz Lady, what do you know about the murder of Joe Blow from Dearborn Heights the other night? You remember him, don't you?

She didn't respond. Instead, her head rolled right and left as light from the rising sun climbed into the room and peeked past the bodies of the detectives who both stood directly in front of her. Just then their bodies shifted, each detective moving a few steps toward the side of the table, and for a brief moment her eyes were riveted by the beauty of the muted sunrise filtering through the grease-stained window.

Sun bothering you? Your eyes are made for the night, right? Well, where were you the night he died? Who were you with? Had you ever been with him before?

I was never with him then. I never seen him before.

Yeah, right.

And so on and so on. Why this, why that. Suddenly the white detective said, Look, bitch, we got witnesses who say that they saw you with him. Then they both left the room as abruptly as they had entered an hour before. Blam, the door shut. She immediately spun her chair around to face it, waiting for their return. She supposed that they would; after all she had waited half the night alone in the interrogation room for them. Surely they had more questions.

She began concentrating on the many dirt smudges on the door in order to distract her from thinking about their return. One smudge, located almost dead center, was long like a snake but with wings like a dragon. Even a plume of pink drifted up from where she imagined the dragon's nose to be. Below it and to the left she saw her mother's full image suspended with yellow daisies in her long dark-brown hair. Her arms were outstretched as if waiting for her sweet little girl to jump into them. This was just the way her mother looked the last time she saw her twenty years ago when she was six. I'll be back for you, baby. I'll be back. And she gave a toss of her head left to right, causing her curly hair to swish right to left. I'll be back for you, baby, the natural mother said while the foster mother held the six-year-old firmly by the shoulders.

Christ, how many times have I seen those detectives cruising the corridor? How many times? They never stopped me before. Actually, one time they had. The black detective was behind the wheel, the white one talked. If she were black, perhaps it would have been the other way around. So, how's business today?

I ain't got no business unless you got some.

He looked over at his partner with a wry grin, then at her. Come on man, she said, leaning into the window. Five dollars. That's all. I can make it worth your while, babee. How bout both of you for seven fifty? My Saturday special.

Get your funky ass outta here.

Come on man, I need the money. They sped off, burning rubber, right down the middle of the corridor. Her lips curled scornfully while she blew a kiss to the retreating car.

This memory, the kiss to the retreating car, elicited at first short puffs of air from her diaphragm. Then recognizable chuckles. Then full-blown, side-splitting laughter. Right there in the interrogation room. Christ. Didn't those two take off? Like bats out of hell.

Suddenly she heard the footsteps of a lone walker approaching the only door to the interrogation room. Her fingers gripped the edge of the chair seat; her left eye rolled to the side and waited for the door to open. It didn't. The footsteps proceeded past the door down the corridor beyond her hearing. Still her left eye remained fixed on the door, waiting for the knob to turn.

Then she began singing softly: Blue Heaven, you know just what I am here for. You heard me say that I prayed for someone I could call my own.

These few words, remembered from a song she used to hear on the radio as a child, were enough to fill both eyes with tears. She wiped her eyes on the edge of the plain gray oversized sweatshirt she wore over black spandex pedal pushers. Why, Mama? Why didn't you return? She took a deep breath. Oh, grow up. With this admonishment to herself she scanned the room for Kleenex or napkins or any piece of paper for her nose. Finding none, she blew into the underside of the same sweatshirt edge she had just used to wipe her eyes. Why did they have to call me a bitch? Then, Hell, what difference does it make now?

Her attention shifted back to the window. She walked over to it and pressed her forehead against a lower pane, adding her body oil to the streaks of grease and dirt that were by now magnified by the full force of the sun. Something was developing across the street at the building advertising Ernie, the bail bondsman. A white man with a dark suit and curly hair conversed with a hefty black woman wearing a hat and carrying a large purse. The woman dabbed her eyes occasionally—a mother. He was a lawyer. Her two teenage daughters gesticulated wildly; at times, one or the other of them would threateningly inch up to the lawyer's face. He didn't budge. Finally, the woman held her right arm out like a traffic cop. Everyone was still for a brief moment. Then she could tell that the lawyer said something because his head leaned toward the woman, then the building. Another brief moment of calm, and the quartet entered the front door.

The gull still tore at the plastic, oblivious to the drama at the curb to its left in front of the bail bondsman's building. By this time, traffic had increased; from the thirteenth floor cars and people looked like dolls moving aimlessly to and fro. Her eyes began darting this way and that in an attempt to keep up with the chaos on the street below.

How brave that bird is. All alone in the middle of the street, all those cars, no other gulls around.

I'll be back, her mother had said, but she never returned. After some time had passed she asked the foster mother why her mother hadn't returned.

Because your mother is a whore. She can't keep you with her, the foster mother said.

What's a whore?

The first one she met on the corridor told her, You gotta get yourself some hair, girl. Then you can do whatever you want; you can be whatever you want.

So she studied every old prostitute in the street, full face, looking into their eyes, feeling their hair. One day, she spotted one parading back and forth on a corner of the lower end of the corridor. Three ragged daisies adorned the prostitute's scraggly brown ponytail.

You must be my mother.

The old prostitute studied her for a moment as if to determine whether or not she was joking. Then, You're crazy. Get away from me. I don't know you.

Later, while working her own corner at the other end of the corridor, she told a prostitute friend, also working that corner, I met my mother. She said that she loves me.

Every day she returned to the same spot at the lower end of the corridor where the old prostitute paraded up and down the curb.

I wear my hair like that, too, sometimes. I must be your daughter.

I said get away from me.

On another day, Why didn't you return for me? I've been waiting all these years for you.

Yet another day, God, I know you're my mother. I just know it.

Why are you picking on me, you crazy Polack bitch. Get the hell away from me. Understand? You ain't mine.

How many times had she heard that word? Fifteen? A thousand? Yet an old prostitute, a toothless hag, her tits sagging to her waist like water-filled balloons, called her a bitch, and the word sounded different.

Have you ever pondered a situation in your life for hours or days or even weeks, reviewing the same moment over and over, the same nodal point at which your life could have turned in another direction? You could be a CEO right now? Right now. You could be a Hollywood star? You could be a happy, respectable homemaker with regular beauty shop appointments and two point five kids? Have you ever studied a moment in your life in detail like that, asking yourself why such and such happened, or why you did this or that? If only you had thought things through then, responded differently? If only, if only? You ask yourself why why why until you have sucked every possible bit of comprehension out of the situation, and your head drops to meet your chest and you find yourself too close to the wall and your head hits. You raise your head, drop it again because you want to bury your thoughts in your chest, sink the whys into your heart, but still you are too close to the wall. Again your head hits. This happens again and again until you ask yourself why? Why can't I even bury my head in my chest? Your head falls against the wall again and again and again until a knot full of the pus of why forms on your forehead?

Surely you understand how she was against the window asking herself why why why? But a window isn't a wall. No one was looking up when she fell. Everyone was either at the corner crossing the street, or entering a building, or looking side to side for a cab. No one saw her enter the corridor from the thirteenth floor to the sidewalk, her body twirling like a ballerina, her hands outstretched, pushing the warm spring air away from her body. No one saw the pale-yellow pearlescent sun or heard the strains of "Blue Heaven" that she hummed to the sky.

Shards of glass from the interrogation room window greeted her on the ground, embedding themselves in her skull. Next the sea gull came over to her body on the sidewalk. The gull walked round and round her even as curious pedestrians began to gather. Several uniformed police officers and the two detectives who had questioned her ran down the steps of the precinct and charged into the crowd. One said after seeing the bloodied gray top and spandex pants, Goddamn bitch must have leaped.

You know how it is when someone falls thirteen floors from any building: the noise, the confusion, the near hysteria of some of the onlookers? The cold curiosity of others? The older woman and her daughters were just leaving the building where the bail bondsman's office was located. They rushed across the street to join the knot of onlookers. She was still alive, but by then her head was nearly flat and on its way to becoming big as the steering wheel of a city bus. The woman put her arms around each one of her girls, who both nestled their head in her neck. Lawd Lawd Lawd, she said. Ummmp ummmp ummmp.

The officers began yelling for the crowd to stand back. There was a disorderly scuttle of feet away from the scene. The gull wandered back to the plastic in the middle of the street. By this time the ambulance siren clearly sounded. With a loud squawk and a furious flap of its wings the gull flew off, leaving the plastic bag containing half a ketchup-soaked hot dog bun.

The teen hanging on to the right shoulder of the woman spotted the bird moments before it squawked, then saw what it left behind as it ascended. Ooh, Mama, look at the nasty shit that gull was eating.

Watch your mouth, girl. You know I don't allow no cussin.

Sorry, Mama.

After briefly removing her thumb from her mouth, the left-side teen said, Well, say what you want, girl, I'm hungry myself. It's been a long morning.

Lawd Lawd Lawd, said the mother as she pulled the girls closer to her. How can you have an appetite at a time like this?

Sadie and Marqway

He loves things of which he has a present need.

—Socrates to Agathon from Plato's *Republic*

Your love is like a state of malnutrition, a murder one
conviction that I can't appeal.

—from "Your Love is a Business Proposition," a song by Leonard King

I.

It was Sadie's first time frying chicken the way her mama does. Grease was spattering all over the stove, on the wall, on the floor, and edges of the chicken were burning. But she had put eggs in the batter to coat the fowl, just like her mama, and tested the grease with droplets of water, just like her mama, so she had every confidence that that chicken would be good for her man, Marqway. Why not? He always liked her mama's.

It was a hot day, too. The kind you wear a muumuu in and only wash your face and armpits. But she also decided to wear lipstick, thick and red and smeared by the time she was midway through frying the stack of legs and wings and thighs in the heat. Who knows why she wore lipstick? He didn't even like it, but she was convinced that red lips were what he really needed, and when you have your man in your heart, you know what's best for him and for you.

So Sadie was frying that chicken and singing "I'm in Love Under New Management" when Marqway appeared at the back door, framed by a few fuzzies from trapped dandelion seeds, a few dead flies and clots of city pollution trapped in the screen door behind him. There he was, tall and slim and darker than usual because at late afternoon on the west side of Detroit, summer sun casts a shadow on the back porch. She almost died. Really. In a way that her heart split in two and felt heavy then fell to her stomach. That's how she died. As she looked through the screen, behind his eyes and saw nothing. She died.

This is what was in her mind—that the chicken's burnt edges and the odor in the kitchen and the muumuu displeased him. But you can't fry chicken in something sexy, and burnt edges could be cut off. Anyone should know that.

Hey, baby, she said. I'm cookin special for you.

He didn't open the door; he didn't step one inch into the kitchen.

It's Saturday, baby, she said again. What we gonna do tonight?

Then she jumped and immediately rushed to the sink. Forget Marqway. Grease had splattered onto the end of her nose. Oh my, it hurt. She shoved aside a mountain of dishes and bowls she had used in preparing the chicken, leaned her head into a space in the deep well-nicked sink, and stuck her nose under the long old-fashioned faucet.

Really, she was under the faucet for only a few seconds, but the water felt so cool and the day was hot and she realized her body was, too. Soon she stuck her whole face under the running cold water. Then she was splashing the top part of herself, including her armpits, and rehashing things. Why did he arrive so early? She was almost finished cooking and would have showered. She would have fixed herself up. She would have had time to cut off the edges of the chicken. If necessary, she would have stripped off the skin and presented the chicken as heart-smart. I'm thinking of you, baby. I'm thinking of our life together.

And she was having fun trying to cook for him. Why did Marqway interrupt that and discover her in such a state? This was what was on Sadie's mind for the few seconds she was under the faucet trying to prevent her nose from becoming a blistering projection six inches above the muumuu.

When she looked up, he was gone.

II.

Dusk rolled into the city, and her brother, DeJuan, tripped into the kitchen through the same back screen door as Marqway. This time the gray dusk hid the screen's imperfections, but mosquitoes darted back and forth, hoping for a way in. One was successful and trailed DeJuan until he plopped down at the kitchen table where Sadie sat lost in thought. But the mosquito chose to land on her neck. DeJuan casually reached over and slapped at it.

Boy, leave me alone.

Oh, excuse me; won't bother me none if that mosquito eats you up.

Sadie passed her hand along the spot DeJuan had slapped and felt the mosquito. She studied the flat, bloody insect now between her index finger and thumb. Shore is a lot of blood. It must have bit some ole big fat person before it tried to get me.

I think that's your blood.

No it ain't.

She felt the spot on her neck. Indeed, the mosquito had bitten her in just that little moment.

At nearly eighteen, Sadie was the surrogate head of the household when her mother wasn't at home. Sixteen-year-old DeJuan was next, and the other two brothers, twelve and ten, brought up the rear. They would mind Sadie; DeJuan would not. Sadie called it his man thing.

You think you know everything, Mr. DeeeJuan. Where you been? You were supposed to be home at five. Ain't it eight now? Mama will want to know about this.

He smiled. So Sadie Mae? Where's Marqway? Nothin ain't happnin today? Or is it tonight? Ah, what a deelight.

Sadie became Sadie Mae when DeJuan linked her to Marqway, her boyfriend for over two years. Mizz Sadie Mae Marqway. That's how he'd taunt her.

Don't call me Sadie Mae. It sounds so country.

You don't mind when Mama calls you that.

That's Mama. So where you been, boy?

Here and there.

Did you get over to the Coney Island?

That wasn't one of my stops.

III.

A mound of chicken sat on a plastic platter on the table, most was still burnt on the edges. A few were totally burnt. An edge of the platter was also deep brown and flaked from sitting too close to the stove burner. A film of grease covered the top layer of chicken, and it was beginning to smell a bit rancid. DeJuan, slouched at the table, suddenly leaned forward and began sorting through the chicken in search of an edible leg or thigh. He didn't have enough patience to be a wing man.

You know, girl, this is some damn good chicken.

Sadie was lost in thought, but a compliment from her brother roused her. You think so? It was my first try. Here, here's a good piece. You want me to fry some potatoes?

He just about inhaled the meat off the leg Sadie offered him then asked her out of the clear blue, the leg dangling from a corner of his mouth like a cigar, Sadie, you ever wonder about our father? I mean you ever wonder about where he is? Is he alive or what? He flicked an invisible ash.

I don't know. I don't know. I don't know, DeJuan. I try not to worry about all that.

I do.

I suppose because you're a boy. She reached over and grabbed a piece of chicken from the top of the pile. It was a wing. She broke off the tip, reserving it for the last. She began to eat the thickest part.

It ain't got nothing to do with being a boy. Don't you wonder? Don't you ask yourself why?

Sadie leaned back into the kitchen chair. I try not to wonder about things I ain't got no control over.

IV.

Rain began falling. It was the kind of rain with no drops to make rhythms; instead it fell as a soft, steady sheet of white noise destined to not last long. It would do nothing to cool the night. DeJuan still picked lazily at edges of the chicken, placing them in his mouth without regard to grease coating or burn. Almost his entire upper torso was stretched out on the table to reach the chicken. Sadie, now slumped in the chair with a small collection of chewed wing bones in front of her, picked at crusts of chicken batter around and under her fingernails. Neither one of them had thought to turn on the radio or the TV or the CD player.

Just then the back gate opened and in a few moments shut. Mama was home. Without exchanging a word with his sister, DeJuan sat straight up, his back flat against the chair. Sadie found herself at the sink, where she began moving dirty dishes around as if she had a plan to wash them. Their mother's thuds up the five steep porch stairs punctuated the rain's white noise. Two youthful male voices taunted each other with a modified and safe version of the dozens. In two well-synchronized leaps they both reached the porch at exactly the same second or so ahead of the mother.

Lawd that rain couldn't wait till we made it from the bus stop? What you two doing? Sadie Mae, what on earth happened in this kitchen?

She was trying to cook, Mama.

You cook something, Sadie? asked Jamal, the youngest brother as he grabbed a wing. What's wrong with this chicken?

There's nothing wrong with it, said Sadie. Mr. DeJuan, with his late-arriving self, has been eating up a storm in here.

The mother threw a quick stern look at DeJuan. What time you get in here, boy?

V.

What a long day for Sadie Mae. She had cleaned the chicken, cooked it, watched her brothers pick through it, then suffered through her mother alternately argue with her brother over his late return home and the mess she had made in the kitchen. She washed dishes then began to scrub the stove, wondering what had happened to her evening with Marqway. Here she was with a house full of family and no Marqway. Her man. The one and only man for her. One day she would marry him, have his babies. Ooh Marqway, where are you now.

Sadie Mae. I say Sadie Mae. You can't dream that stove clean. Put some elbow grease into it. I ain't never seen such a mess just to cook. I'm tempted to keep you out of this kitchen forever. How you think you'll get a man keeping a dirty kitchen like this? Well maybe you can get him, but you sure can't keep him.

Sadie swiveled around. Is that what happened to our father? A dirty kitchen?

DeJuan stood straight up. The boys scurried over to him. The mother, her eyes slit, her head shifting from one side to the other, glared at Sadie. There was the longest moment of silence, dead silence, measured by steady, warm rain, still pounding the sidewalk, the back porch and soaking the screen door.

Finally, her mother said, I'm tired, and ambled off, not looking left or right, to the bedroom to retire for the evening. The two youngest boys followed without a word. The kitchen became quiet again. DeJuan slumped on the table again. Again he picked at the few remaining pieces of chicken.

VI.

Sadie was still at the kitchen sink when DeJuan bolted up from the table and ran out of the screen door. Normally, Sadie would have rushed after him to call him back, question where he was going, and so on. This time she kept her head down, giving the cast iron skillet she had fried the chicken in a long and rough scrub of the Brillo pad.

What's the use? A few tears dribbled down and then a few more and then she succumbed to a deep cry. Remembering and remembering things. She began remembering how each one of her brothers came home from the hospital. There was a big celebration for DeJuan's arrival. Aunts and uncles and neighbors arrived to view the new addition. Her mother was so tired and sitting in a corner of the same kitchen Sadie was standing in now. The baby passed around from woman to man to woman to man. The oohs and ahs and all that. Drinks and so on. She, yes she, went over to her father and asked, Did y'all do this for me?

He, in the opposite corner of the kitchen from her mother, bleary-eyed and tucked in a nest of men, all of them toasting with brown liquid, said, What you mean, baby girl?

Did y'all celebrate when I was born?

Of course we did, baby girl. We danced when you was born cuz we knew you was the prettiest little thing we had ever seen. You was the most beautiful creature on earth. Yes, Lawd. Yes, Lawd. And he began to dance, shaking his hips this way and that.

VII.

The rain picked up, still with no promise of cooling the night. Sadie's eyes had dried. She was now sitting at the table staring vacuously at a fly buzzing in the grimy upturned light fixture hanging from the ceiling. The muumuu was greasier and the lipstick was gone, only a faint hint of pink remained, revealing the outer edges of her thin lips. Over and over she replayed the words "baby girl" and "beautiful creature" in her mind. She was trying to remember the sound of her father's voice and the exact color of his skin. She had one picture of him cradling DeJuan in his arms. It was crumpled and faded. All of the other pictures of him had escaped the house. There were no pictures of her two younger brothers' father.

There were few pictures of any of them. Maybe one or two of her mother when she was young and a picture of her mother's other man, long dead. There were no pictures on the walls, except in the younger boys' bedroom, where they had hung pictures of cartoon heroes and cars from magazines. There were no crayon drawings from school. Wait a minute, yes, in her mother's bedroom, a small collection of Mother's Day and Valentine cards made by each one of them at school.

DeJuan had been standing at the screen door for nearly ten minutes before Sadie noticed him. She was that lost in reverie about crayon cards to their mother, none to their fathers. Sadie and DeJuan's eyes locked, his face smashed against the screen, his full lips laced by raindrops caught on the screen.

Oooo boy, you look ugly like that.

Not as ugly as your boyfriend Marqway looks right now.

VIII.

Their wuz nots and wuz toos filled the late-night kitchen. DeJuan insisting that Marqway was killed at the Coney Island because he was spittin at this chick.

Marqway spit at someone? By this time the mother was standing in the doorway between the living room and the kitchen. He was killed for spitting on someone? That doesn't even sound like Marqway? And why couldn't she just spit back?

His mother's question caused DeJuan to launch into side-splitting laughter. He could barely explain to her that spittin meant hitting on. Talking to a young lady. And that is something Marqway ain't never done to Miss Sadie Mae. He used to just come here to eat your chicken, Mama.

Right away Sadie stepped long, reached out, and slapped DeJuan. The mother ran to grab Sadie, who had begun to sob. He's disrespecting Marqway. That man ain't never cared for anyone but me. Mama, how could he say lies like that on Marqway? I don't even believe Marqway is dead. I'm going to see for myself.

Don't bother, Sadie, said DeJuan, The body is gone now.

Indeed, Johnny's Coney Island was closed by then; yellow tape around the entranceway marked it as a police crime scene. Witnesses to the shooting were already saying to friends and neighbors that the restaurant's owner was there when the shooting occurred and that, for whatever reason, he had locked the doors to the restaurant as soon as the gunman fired the last of five shots and fled. It was another half hour or so before he even called the police and more time before they arrived and then the ambulance. Marqway had bled to death.

Sadie's sobs abated long enough for her to ask DeJuan this series of questions. Did you see him? Do they know who shot him? Who was he supposed to be talkin to?

Naw, I don't know anything. It was all over by the time I got there. I'm just telling what folks was sayin about how it all went down.

The mother pulled Sadie to her, and the child buried her head in her mother's chest and sobbed again, all the while wondering what time the shooting occurred because Marqway sure as anything had come by to see her that afternoon while she was cooking chicken for him. And she had kept cooking for him all afternoon. Maybe while she was cooking chicken, even the last batch, he lay dying. She recalled how he hadn't said anything to her. Maybe he was dying then when she was cooking the first batch. He didn't know, and she didn't know that all the chicken in the world wouldn't save him.

Adios, Detroit

Dear Mama:

What I want most is a plate full of red beans and rice and a good Bogey movie. Maybe Clark Gable. Maybe a movie with Bogey and Clarky. Wasn't there one like that? How about a movie with Humphrey Bogart and Clark Gable and Spencer Tracy and Lauren Bacall? We could look at Bogey through sultry eyes the way Lauren did. Or get red in the face when Gable stared out at us with that bad-boy look of his. Did you get hot when you watched those movies? I did a little in my young girl way. I don't know if I would now or not. True, I know what a woman could feel if she could feel, I just don't know if I can feel anything anymore. Not today. Okay, if Valentino were to walk in here this minute, I might feel a quiver.

I wonder what you must have felt then in front of the television on the edge of your seat. Were you panting inside, Mama? I think that I am beyond that now, but you must have had that much in you then, didn't you? A pant or two for handsome Hollywood men? I never saw you breathe heavily, but something must have been happening. Why else would you hurry and cook rice and beans on Sunday afternoons in time to catch Bill Kennedy. You ate your rice with grace as you would say, mixing bits of stew beef in with each mouthful, dropping rice grains on the carpet. There were the two of us in the living room in front of the television with heaping plates of food, my father and Cyrilla in the kitchen to eat by themselves. That's one thing the both of them had in common, a dislike for television. I'm not too particular myself for television in general, but on Sundays when it's cold and the snow blows, I feel as if I could eat a good set of red beans and rice, stew beef, and watch one of those old-time Hollywood boys ooze sexiness on the screen.

To Cyrilla:

This is what memory is for me: fantasy and time. Me locked in closets of dream for as long as I dare, and when I awake, I am saying to myself: oh this is real—the closet, the dream. The cold air nipping at my nose is not for real. The sun and the birds flying high in its heat are not for real. Their wings will melt in the sun like Icarus, then they will land on the sidewalk, flat and lifeless. Even then they are not real unless I can close my eyes and see them, reconstruct them, blow air into them, hang them in the sky like a mobile.

Do you realize that in the Catholic Church my birth is on the feast of the Ascension? In history it is the date the first atom bomb was dropped? I think about these things and wonder if anything I try to do in life matters. I would like to soar but someone or something drops bombs on my head. I am like a bird with melted wings.

I wish you could understand. Who else should or could? Why tell anyone you ask? Because I am tired of feeling so tight, C. As if cold, rough iron lodges in my bowels. I can't bend over; I can't lean back. If I want to twist this way, I groan in pain. If I want to twist that way, same thing. Christ, Cyrilla, my life so far has been one long search for a good purge. Do you understand what I mean? Remember when we used to have to take castor oil and then senna the week before Easter and the week before Christmas? Remember how nasty they tasted, but how clean we felt after, especially when Mama pronounced us fit enough to eat a good set of Easter and Christmas sweets?

Cyrilla, I long for a good cleansing. What do you think I should do? Really? Should I holler on the street corner? Should I drop my drawers and swing my bam bam over the new dumpster Coleman Young installed in the alley behind my house? Should I drop my own atom bomb out there behind the house with cats and rats watching? Should I conduct my own purge?

I would like to ask you just once if you experienced the same as me. I would feel ashamed if it were only me that he was feeling up. No real father would do that. If anything, I am convinced he wasn't my real father because of his actions. I swear to you, Cyrilla, that I would forget about this thing if I could only know the truth from you. This thing is like a rock on my neck, but I can free myself. I know that I can free myself. All it takes is willpower to say: turn your head another way. Look to the horizon. Don't look back; look forward.

In truth, I've been jealous of you for as long as I can remember. You've been in the middle of a life I have been observing from the fringes. The real reason I am too afraid to talk to you in person about this matter is that I don't want to open the Pandora's box. What if you say, "He never touched me." What if you say, You are lying, Mida. Either one of those two statements would be a wedge between us. Even though I realize that if you said that he didn't touch you, then he didn't touch you. Even though I realize that if I told you the truth, you would be hurt. You had no more control over life than I did. What can I say? There is a loneliness in me, C. It is in my guts. Deep, deep in there.

There have been years when I didn't think about anything more than how to get out of the bed, how to go to work, how to cook dinner when I returned home. Years before that I thought about nothing except how to dodge my husband. Years before that I thought about nothing except schoolwork. Years and years, C, until now and this piece of paper, this substitution for you. This paper doesn't have the same warmth as you. It's cold and white; you are like fire. Even when you cheups me. Especially when you are angry at me and pout. Even when you call me pendeja. I would like so much to hear you call me a liar to my face, but I don't have the courage to say what needs to be said.

What brings all of this on? A man at work. A little chupid, drunken man. He means nothing, but he said something. He was out of line at the wrong time of the month for me, the wrong time of the day.

Not the first time a chupid drunken man has been out of line. But this is the first time at the wrong time of my life. So here I am spilling my wounded guts to a sheet of paper, calling it you. I kissed you two paragraphs ago, my darling big sister. But when my lips lifted from you, they were dry.

To my father:

We were just over to see you yesterday. Ramona and I came with silk flowers, three anthuriums and some white lilies. I buy them at a little flower shop on the east side. They are awfully expensive, but it's the only place I know to get silk anthuriums. The lady there calls me when the weather turns cold and the silk flowers arrive. I go buy anthuriums immediately and wait until it's time to see you.

I don't know what I thought your gravestone could tell me about events above ground, but that is partly what I wanted to find out from you. Do you know the smell in Mama's house? It was there a few weeks ago. This is your former home. Do you know anything at all? Mama has assured Cyrilla and me that you would not come to her with an odor but as a dream or a vision, neither of which you have done yet. She is still waiting to hear from you. I think it grieves her that you haven't appeared to her at all, that you haven't given her a sign that all is well. If the spirits intended one, wouldn't they send it?

We've suffered enough with your death, so unexpected, so crazy. Those days immediately following as we prepared for the funeral, Mama repeated often that this country is cold and hard. But, Mama, it's big summertime that he has died. Both Cyrilla and I said this. She said that summer in this country is not true hot sun. There is for her always the memory of the last winter.

Yes, she is upset that she hasn't heard from you. Am I the only one who has? I found myself in one long dream last night. In the end I tried to make fry bakes for you. I suppose I believed that you had come to me in the dream to tell me that everything would be alright, that no man would make me unhappy again. But the bakes didn't come out so good; I threw them out. Come to think of it, perhaps it is best that the bakes weren't that good because then I would have really been upset. She doesn't say it so much, but it's the way she talks about you still, hoping that everything is okay with you and hoping that you ended up in a good place. Do you think that your silence makes her believe you ended up in hell? To tell you the truth, even though Mama says that the smell could not come from the dead, it passed my mind that maybe a dead in hell would stink.

My daughter was with me this trip to your grave so I was unable to ask you a few other things that have been lingering in my mind since your death. For example, now that you are where you are, on the other side of this life, what do you think of your life when you were on this side? I won't say that you are in heaven or hell now because I don't believe in a specific place for life ever after. I don't even know if I believe in life ever after except that when I go to your grave, I feel compelled to speak to you as if your spirit is around to respond. Where else could you be? Not at my house because I bought it after you died. You have never seen it. At Cyrilla's?

Ah girl, you too fussy, nuh. You let every little ting bodder you.

At Mama's? You too grown to worry about such foolishness.

You know what they give. I don't want to be the one to judge you by saying that you should be in one spot or the other in the spirit universe, but at the grave is where I feel your spirit.

I wanted to ask you if you have memory now? Is it permitted where you are at? It's difficult for me to imagine life or death without memory burning my brain. You know how memory is. It can be no more than a few words and a half-image. Or it can be a long movie with a cast of thousands, a complete musical score, intermission, bathroom breaks, and popcorn. Sometimes my memory is at night when I sleep. I have crazy dreams and wake up crying or sweating. Sometimes my memory is on the back of my eyelids. I close them and see myself in a closet and all the sounds around me are muffled laughs. I am completely alone. Then again there are times when I am washing dishes in the house that I live in now and suddenly I feel a set of lips on the back of my neck and hands on my breast. I swivel around, but only the cat is perched on top of the refrigerator door staring at me.

After death almost everyone is a hero, created by the memory of the last good live moment and the last glance at the casket. Your body snuggled in white looked pitiful and lonely, everyone staring at you as if you were a freak. I remember that, and that alone erases everything else I may have wanted to cling to. Not really. I have been holding on to things that I should have let go of right then and there in the direct presence of your death. I should have been grabbing for my own life right then and there. Let go of you, held on to me.

The other day, a gentleman asked me if I was a poet. Should I have told him that when you died I menstruated for thirty days straight? Or should I have told him, no, I'm not a poet but a woman who bleeds.

Making Callaloo

But nobody paid attention to the tale, because
the sun was traveling from East to West and the
hours which grow on the right-hand of clocks must
become longer out of laziness since they are those
which lead most surely to death.

—Alejo Carpentier, "Journey to the Seed," translated by Jean Franco

Bush was everywhere in the house, beginning from a crack at the side
door, and it was cold outside. I never saw anything like this. Bush was
hanging from the ceiling, coming up from the cracks in the wooden
floors, snaking round from behind the archway leading to the kitchen.
Coiled round the banister leading to upstairs. I could only imagine the
bush had taken over up there, too. But the house was dark and things
were thick, and I didn't care to work my way up the stairs just then.
In the same way, I didn't feel to work my way through to the kitchen,
especially since the leaves had formed such a nice thick carpet, too

nice for my footprints, even though by this time I had taken off my boots and was still in the vestibule in my stocking feet. It was snowing outside, and I had one hell of a time coming to her house in all that mess. But I needed to see her.

From where I stood in the vestibule just inside the front door, I could well see the side door and the vine coming into the house from under it. I suppose I could have gone outside and round the house to the side to check for sure, but I didn't feel like putting on my boots again. I would check on the way out.

Just then Tante's soft and crackly voice said, Come let me chalk yuh foot, dahlin. It's been a long time since I've seen you.

She see I ent move. Come in. Come in. I've been waiting for you.

By this time my eyes still had not adjusted to the darkness, but to me as if I saw an anthurium growing up from a corner by the fireside. Then I realized it was some kind of silky silky fake thing she must have put there since the last time I was by to see her. Things change. In all my born days I don't remember her having fake flowers or plants in her house. Then again, I don't remember her having live ones. She was an outdoor lady for gardening. Every time I came to see her in summer she toured me through the yard to show off the roses and bleeding hearts and other bright petals and to show off tomato plants, and one year we stopped at a little spot right by the steps to her side door, the brightest spot in her yard, where she had planted a piece of dasheen, and you could see the bush growing thick and healthy right there on the northwest side of Detroit in a little piece of tough dirt. This town ent never seen anything like this, she bragged.

I bet you're right.

So I realized this dark big-leaf thing that had taken over her house had to be the dasheen bush, and I didn't know what to make of this. Dasheen bush doesn't grow like vine. Still, things change. Who knows what they do these days to provisions. They does mix up things however they want. But how they could make dasheen bush come like this? Like a grapevine? Maybe Tante self did something to it.

This reminds me of my friend's philodendron. I have been to her house several times and have seen the plant climbing from the pot via a trellis then finding its way along the path she set up for it. I saw the same thing in a boutique the other day. It was one of those places that sells candles and whatnots, and the philodendron vines gave it an air of mystery, although I must admit that there were scarcely any leaves and the vine looked scraggly. It needed trimming back to thicken it up, but some people don't want to realize that sometimes you have to make these sacrifices in order to have something better in the end.

Not so in Tante's house. She must be trimming this bush like crazy, because everywhere I looked it was as if I was in the tropics. Everything was thick thick thick and steamy like a jungle. Like what they does call de bush over on the island where she came from. I was beginning to wonder how she could breathe in all this. I heard the other day you musn't sleep with too much green plants in your room; they poison the air. And here I grew up thinking that green plants give you clean air by using the carbon dioxide you breathe out. Now they're saying not to have any plants in the bedroom, don't carry plants when visiting the sick, and so on. I was sure the bush was in Tante's room, so I was wondering how she could breathe while sleeping. Even how she could breathe downstairs because, if I could draw you a picture of how much crisscrossing of vines there was in this place, you would be shocked. I was wondering how she could even move around in there.

I myself had not budged an inch since I opened the front door. And when I heard her voice saying for me to come in, I still didn't move.

I now come to realize I couldn't even see her. And since she called out for me to enter, I hadn't heard a word from her. So I called out, Tante? Tante?

Yes, baby. Is then I catch how the voice was really tired sounding, almost as if to cry.

Tante, you OK?

Yes, child.

It was still taking a long time for my eyes to adjust to the darkness, but to me as if I saw a few strands of silver a way back in the living room off to the right from where I was standing. Could be Tante's hair, I said to myself. What else could it be? Normally there was a little table with curios in that corner, an arrangement of porcelain cats and dancing ballerinas. So I began looking to see if I could catch a glow from her eyes. I figured if I see the hair, then I should see the eyes soon enough. I ent see nothing. Tante, you there?

Look me here nuh, child.

Still I can't see her. By this time so I don't want to seem as if I'm chupid, so I make like I'm taking off my coat and making small talk prior to coming into the living room. Tante, my mouth feel for callaloo. Is a long time since I had any real callaloo. Now I was ready to put my coat in the closet right there in the vestibule. It was the first time I ever thought to put my coat in the front closet. Usually I came in by the side door. Usually I went as far as the kitchen. Usually I throw my coat over a chair in the dining room or over the back of a kitchen chair. Things change. She had a set of junk outside on the path leading to the side door. I figured she was cleaning house and maybe someone was coming to remove it. Tante always had a set of young boys and men coming to remove or install something. Her husband died so many years ago. She could very well do for herself way back then, you know, but now that she is older she needs help with pounding nails and moving heavy things and so on. Now and again when I come by, I even help her clean up a few little things. But it's been so long. How she have all this bush inside the place here?

I can't open the door to the closet. I pull and I push, push and pull. The damn door still won't open. Is how it hasn't opened in so long, I figure. I push and pull again, trying to be so quiet. I don't want to arouse her suspicion. You know how folks are about their homes? Sensitive? They don't want you to find any fault with anything in their homes. Times before if I would say something like, Hey, Tante, this chair is looking a little unstable. You want me to see if I can fix it for you? I think a bit of glue here would do the trick.

Nothing is wrong with that chair, nuh. You gain some weight? Just the other day Mr. Ting was here and he ent find no fault with the chair.

Case closed. You see why I was afraid to say anything about the door? She well pick me up the other day about the chair. So it was better for me to stand by the door, holding my coat in my hand. I even thought about putting the coat back on, but it was hot for so in there, even by the door where a little of the January cold could seep in. The other thing is, if I put my coat back on, she would think I ent come for a real visit, to sit down and ole talk for a while. I don't want to make her feel bad. So I figure I would hold my coat in my hand and when I get in there, I would throw the coat over a chair in the living room or even sit in the dining room because I never used to throw a coat in the living room or even sit in the living room because her living room was always clean like a whistle and nobody ever sat in there. It was just for show. But things change, you know. Now the living room has so much bush in it I don't even know if I can get through. I was wondering if this coat would hold me back. I might need both my hands to push through. Something like Indiana Jones hacking his way through jungles.

Oh Lord. Now my mind is really leaving me. But Tante well liked the Indiana Jones man, you know. Even more so she loved Waylon Jennings. His voice thrilled her. Myself, I ent see nothing in him. Before when I came by she would be listening to him on the TV or on the radio. Waylon Jennings. What kind of name is that? Then I would come in and see her doing some kind of hokey-pokey thing and singing, We closing in on the fire. We reaching up; we reaching down. We burning up; we burning down. And I would say to myself, What is this atall? This is weird. This old island woman dancing hokey-pokey to Waylon Jennings? What kind of name is that?

Then I would think this man must be her Mr. Ting. In all the time I was coming by to see her, I never met Mr. Ting. I ent even know his name. All the time she was calling him Mr. Ting. Make me believe he didn't really exist. Still she would give concrete details. He was so and so tall, dark hair, sexy eyes. That's why I think Mr. Ting was only in her imagination. Then again how could she be telling me about Mr. Ting sitting in the chair and so on? Unless she's well crazy? Or lonely? What Doudou?

All this time so I'm still fumbling with this blasted coat, shifting it from arm to arm. Finally I let it slip to the floor and with my foot stuffed it in the corner of the vestibule. There, that was done. I could begin to find my way into the living room. Still I couldn't see clearly enough to just walk in, and, too, I couldn't figure out how to pass through the vines hanging right there in the archway without breaking a leaf. I could even break off a whole long piece if I didn't pass through gently. Now I'm not fat, but I couldn't figure how I could fit through the little slits of space in the tangle. These vines were hanging right down to the floor. Actually, I would have to lift my leg and climb through the one spot with an opening possibly big enough for me to pass. So this is what I began to do and immediately got caught in the vines. I couldn't even get my foot on the floor on the other side of the vines, the floor of the living room itself. Oh God, now what to do? I stood there for minutes with my right leg cocked up over the cluster of vines. I made several attempts to thrust myself forward so I could hop into the living room but nearly fell backward. Fortunately, I managed to catch myself by placing my left hand against the closet door. I pulled my leg back through and planted it on the vestibule floor. What a mess.

What you doin there gyul?

Nothing, Tante. I'm just looking for something in my purse.

What? What you have there you looking so hard for?

Nothing really. I think I may have left my car keys in the car. I hope I didn't lock them up in there.

You going already?

Is the same thing I didn't want her to think, that I was leaving already. I'm so chupid sometimes. Why did I have to say something about car keys? I could have told her anything else. O gosh no, Tante. I'm just checking. I'm coming right in to visit. I comin, nuh, Tante.

All in a sudden she calling out, Doudou? Doudou?

I play along with she. Yes, Cocots.

Doudou?

Yes, Cocots. Dahlin Cocots.

Kômâ ou jodi?

Biê, Cocots. Biê.

Doudou? Allé. Poté pip. Alimé pou mwê. Mwê vlé fimê.

O gosh, I can't carry she the pipe. Me ent got none. All in a sudden I hear she belch. One long loud belch, like a man working on the docks. Buhhhhhhhh. Oh gosh, I never hear anything like this before. Then she say, Doudou, mwê faim. Moit vlé pwasô é pi diri.

Cocots, sa mwê piti callaloo. I shoulda known she hungry. Who feeding she all this time? Where is she? O God, nuh. I looking all around me like a pierrot grenade and I realize all I have is the bush. Is then I begin picking the bush self. What was I to do? I ent think to bring food for she. Of course she hungry. Who been feeding she? O gosh, how could I be so chupid?

I drop my purse and pick pick pick the leaves all around the archway. Me ent even know what to do with the leaves. When I ever make callaloo? I only eat it when Tante or Mummy makes it. How I going to make callaloo now in someone else's kitchen? I don't know my way around she kitchen. But I pick pick pick the leaves. As I picking, I seeing a way clear to where she's at, and my eyes are now accustomed to the darkness. She's lying there with her hand down between she legs.

What the hell? What going on here I say to myself? Then she start singing "Closing the Fire." We reaching up; we reaching down.

Then all in a sudden I smell something stink. As if a sore foot. Maybe I smellin my top lip? But in truth this is stink beyond top lip. Like a dead cat or dog lying around.

Tante, you all right?

Oh, he did love me so. Never, never, never a man love me so.

I wondering who she's talking about. Waylon Jennings? Mr. Ting? She husband? No, he dead so long ago. She can't be thinking about him. Then she laughs, a crazy cackling.

Tante? Tante?

This. This.

What she mean, this? This what? All now I'm standing with my hands full of the leaves. I ent know what to say. Here I am looking at my aunt lying on the couch with she hands poking around between she legs. To besides I seeing a dydee on her. Is that the this she talking about? What de arse?

Tante, Tante? What going on here. Look I coming to help. I'll be making callaloo for you to eat.

I know you. I know you. You are . . .

Yes, Tante. Yes, Tante. Is me.

O ho. Yes, is you. Yes, Doudou, dohn bother coming nuh. Look me muddah and me faddah is here already. All dem is here. Me tante and all dem is here. They bring me a big set a callaloo. Just how I like it. A big piece a salt pork floating in de ting. No child. I'm all set. We all here going down on this callaloo. Is a long time since I see all these folks here. But I have a feeling we'll be sharing this callaloo for a long time, gyul. A long time. It's OK, you know. All dem is here. No child, dohn worry to come again. I'm OK, you know. Dohn worry. You dohn worry.

I stood there couyont in truth, my hands full of the leaves. Is now I'm wondering what to do with them. I ent have no salt pork, no crab, no nothing, and here she is already talking about eating this callaloo.

Over the Belle Isle Boundary

All of the Antilles, every island, is an effort of memory; every mind, every racial biography culminating in amnesia and fog. Pieces of sunlight through the fog and sudden rainbows, *arcs-en-ciel*. That is the effort, the labour of the Antillean imagination, rebuilding its gods from bamboo frames, phrase by phrase

—Derek Walcott, "The Antilles, Fragments
of Epic Memory," Nobel Lecture

It was a hot-sun and breezeless day. Solar rays pressed relentlessly against the fourth-floor nursing home window facing East Grand Boulevard. The home really had no recourse from the sun in its treeless section of what was called convalescent row only a spit north of Belle Isle. The rays penetrated the panes, boldly thrusting themselves far down the hall, some almost to the utility room. Some reached just to the nursing station, located midway on the floor, weaving over and under papers and medications on the countertop. Others preferred to linger on the edge of the bare ceiling-almost-to-floor window where all of them had entered. Some settled by the exit door just by the window. But one wide and gentle ray curled around the corner of the first resident room where it crept up on the bed of a sleeping fawn-colored old man and flopped across waiting for him to rouse.

As it waited, strands of it began wrapping around the old man's toes and his fingers and caressing his lightly whiskered face. He whispered ooooh aahhh and rubbed crusty eyes where the sands of sleep lodged; he hadn't been bathed yet. He passed his hands up and down his cheeks and for no reason at all called out softly to his wife, the woman he called Mummy in life and in death, and she called him shuga-plum. She had been wife and mother to him and was good to their only child, a son who had become a world traveler; Lord in heaven knows where he is now. Mummy, you see how I come? Dog betta den me.

But if Mummy were alive, not even she could have understood his stroke-slurred speech, further hampered by a tongue lightly purpled and slightly swollen from lack of use. The stroke took him quick and left him slumped and drooling in a pool of his own urine in the stairwell of the building he migrated to after his wife died. Tang God for the man who came by and found him.

Mummy would have said, Tang God, but that's not what he thought through stroke-laced brain waves as the ambulance personnel arrived to carry him off, Oh Mummy, how could you leave me like this?

Then as they strapped him on the stretcher, O Lorse take me now, he silently pleaded with the heavens.

I comin Mummy as the ambulance rolled toward Henry Ford Hospital. I comin by you.

But he didn't meet Mummy then. The medical staff kept him from her, tidied him up and released him to the nursing home, where he hasn't spoken one single intelligible word to one living soul since, except for silent prayers to his Mummy, beseeching her to come for him. He spoke not an intelligible word to the rotating staff that fed him the nursing home pap through his feeding tube and changed his dydee after feeding, not to the head nurse who often came in to pinch his big toe for a sign of life. In response he would grunt words she couldn't understand, What de arse you want in here now? To the Catholic priest who came weekly to pray with him, he moaned. But he communicated fluently to the motes that swirled around in his room on sunny days as he mumbled messages for them to carry to Mummy.

More awake now he blinked; the sun was so bright, Wait, nuh, where am I? Is as if, wait, nuh; where de hell am I? He asked a cluster of dust that settled on the back of the wide sunray; then he slipped into a dream of pelau on beach Sunday and the crab he would catch between platefuls of the rice dish. He was seeing himself in this dream, nice and slim and handsome catching the eye of a young Mummy rushing out to meet the waves at Mácuri Beach, between his legs getting hot as he chased after her, and just then a crab came from nowhere and bit his toe.

What are you smiling at, old man? It was the nurse pinching his toe. He cheups. Why de arse she can't leave me alone?

She scanned the room as he eyed her through slits. Ah chut, what she want now? Then he drifted off again to rejoin Mummy on the beach; she was dishing out the pelau, and he was holding a bottle of peppa sauce waiting to dash it on the rice. It was he and Mummy for so long. She giving the peppa; he getting the sauce. And now he was on this bed in this shit-ass nursing home waiting to rejoin Mummy.

All in a sudden the dream shifted to the dusty yard of his boyhood home in Oronuevo Village. His brother Toli comes along with a flat stick whittled from the coconut tree in the front of their house and running up to him is their friend Alfonso, bowling a ball he had fashioned from a rock and some twine. Toli hit the ball, but Winston, another friend from down the road, picks it up, pivots magnificently, and breaks the wicket. Well played, bhai, Alfonso yells out to Winston. Well played. Yuh finally break a wicket, bhai. The three of them, all early teenagers, smile big at the sexual innuendo and wave at the old man. Then Toli says, You're up brother, and the old man, who appears in his youth, is now batting. He is younger than Toli and taller; Toli is fairer; both are slim. Alfonso turns his back to the old man in the bed and begins running toward the young man, chest thrust forward, head high, ball in his right hand, left touching it, and almost leaps into the air to begin the hand-over-hand movements that add thrust to the bowl. Perfect, perfect. Yes, buddy, I can well remember those days as if they were yesterday.

The Young Terrors of Oronuevo consisted of eleven regulars and a few alternates. Both he and Toli batted, they were usually in partnership. Toli was a better batsman. In truth, Toli was better than him all-around in cricket. Winston Ramkeeson and Alfonso Luces from the other side of the junction practiced cricket with them in the front yard morning, noon, and night when school was out. They played at school during recess and after school. Alfonso was their star bowler, but they all switched up batting and bowling and playing the field. Winston was another all-around player. At any one point, one of them might brag after a good play, Walcott ent have nuteeng on us, yuh know. Yes, cricket is a sunshine game, and a hot-sun day like today always reminded the old man of airborne bowlers, broken wickets, and dramatic overs.

Yes buddy, is a nice game, nuh, a nice game. Oh what I wouldn't give to see dose boys again Toli, Alfonso, and Winston. It was eleven of dem in all. Dey made deir own pitch right dere to practice in front de yard and made the wicket from that same coconut tree. Well in de first place since cricket is played with two persons at de same time against all eleven of de other team, Toli and me were de lead batsmen. So whoever was de bowler would bowl to us first. You hit the ball, and according to the distance you hit the ball you can make one run or two runs, or three runs or four if it roll on the ground and hit one of the boundary. When Toli hit that ball and it go over the boundary, that's a six. It's a game you really have to understand, but it is a real nice game.

He tried many times to explain the game to Detroit people, but they never understood.

Yes, buddy, three men, six wickets; three wickets on this end and three on the other end, no two wickets and six stumps. Yes, that's it. And when the bowler hits the wicket, that man is out; and he hits the ball and it goes up in the air and it didn't go far enough and one of the fielders pitching, that man is out; and if he hit the ball and don't ah if he hit the ball . . . what the hell am I talking about?

Just then his eyes flew open, fully connecting him with buzzing activity in the hallway just outside of his room. While the sun played with the old man and he followed the shadows dancing across his memory, the nursing staff bustled up and down the hall, stepping over rays, walking right through them, completely oblivious as they cleaned every corner and reorganized this and that in anticipation of a surprise walk-through visit from the State Certification Board. Mainly, they wanted the joint to smell good so bouquets of silk flowers sprayed with a potpourri scent appeared everywhere to brighten things up and help camouflage the urine odor that had sunk into the walls, under the paint, and behind the baseboards. Every staff practiced sporting a wide smile while changing the loaded dydees of old and forgotten souls, vacant faces with drooling mouths. Staff cooed lovingly to them as if they were newborn darlings, deftly cleaned bottoms, switched stained or heavy dydees for fresh ones, and then made airplane noises to the darlings as encouragement to eat the colorless pap that would soon refill the dydees.

Not one hint of urine smell would escape from this home on this Sunday morning, certainly not on the fourth floor where staff prided itself on being the most efficient and most attentive team in the entire building. Staff squirted extra deodorizer in corners along the bed edges, in utility closets, and wherever used dydees congregated.

A young woman staffer, starched and pleasant with hair slicked into a neat little bun, entered the old man's room, brushing past the section of the sunray that hugged the doorframe. She quickly arrived at his bedside at the point the ray began its ascent to the bed. Whistling an elevator tune through bright red lips, she stepped directly on it, startling the old man. He squinted up at her. She smiled cheerily at him.

Good morning, Sweetie.

It was the last day of her first week of employment there, and her first solo dydee change. But with eight brothers and sisters under her, she had performed enough diaper changes to feel absolutely confident that she could handle this resident. In addition, she had received a day's worth of training on the art of changing adults.

Still, she wondered if the coming weeks would find her searching for another job. The nursing home, where her mother had worked for years, was hopefully a temporary stop for her on the way to community college and later maybe university. She wanted to be a doctor or a lawyer, someone successful, anyone but an aide in a nursing home where she was beginning to realize old people steal whatever years they can from young people. Look, in only one week some of her aged. She certainly felt it. How could she enjoy her youth looking at those old faces every day?

Come on, Sweetie, It's time to clean you up. She patted him on his arm, while surveying the room to see what she would need for his sponge bath.

By this time, the old man's reverie took him down East Grand Boulevard to Belle Isle. That's where he and his wife spent many summer Sundays observing cricket matches with others from the small West Indian community in Detroit. Mummy would carefully wrap a cast iron pot full of pelau in an old dish towel, lovingly securing the four corners of the towel with a large safety pin. She would nest a couple of avocados in the corner of the picnic basket, along with peppa sauce, sweet cakes, and utensils. Others would bring fruits, rum and sweet drinks, ice, cookies, chips, and so on. One time someone brought a manual ice cream maker, and everyone took turns churning. But always his loving wife would bring the pelau, her specialty, long-recognized as the best in the Detroit island community.

Ah those were the days, when the cricket teams would come in from all over-Windsor, for sure, and as far as Chicago. Toledo and all had a team back then. All those brown bodies clad in white flannel and white shoes on the green field. They bowled and batted, broke wickets, and often sent balls way over the boundary of the cricket field by the Casino to shouts of Well played, bhai, well played.

When the cricketers took a break for liquids and food, the fans gathered at the picnic tables clustered across a small path east of the field. The men dribbled peppa sauce on platefuls of pelau, drank the rum straight with lime, and rehashed the innings just played.

When fielders returned to the field, and batsmen and bowlers returned to the pitch, the fans retook their positions on the bleachers by the riverside to cheer all of the players on without real team allegiance; after all they were now all citizens of this island in this city. So, they shouted out appropriately to whichever team: Good running or cool down, bhai, cool down. It's a bowler's game.

Well maybe luck's allowed, maybe, maybe. I'll be able to go to Belle Isle one of dese days to see another game. Yeah, buddy. Yeah. Yuh run with de bat when one guy hit de ball he's going to run to try and score as many runs as he can. It depends on how hard yuh hit de ball; if yuh hit it real hard, it go over the boundary; that's a six. If yuh don't reach to de end, dey run yuh out; dey call it runout. Some of dem bhais can't make it. Dey try to make one run and sometimes dey don't; dey don't make it. Den dey want to make two runs and so on. And when one guy hit de ball and he don't hit it hard enough and he hit it in front of one of de fielders and he have to run with de bat in he hand and he run, run, and what the hell, yes buddy, run, run.

And he began groaning. Whan go, whan go, whan go.

What, Sweetie?

Louder and louder. Whan go, whan go, whan go.

Was he speaking some foreign language, fragments of a tribal vocabulary that had been suppressed over the years? And then the stroke problem? She turned to find the head nurse. She wanted to know where this man was from. Maybe she could figure out a way to understand him if she knew the language he was speaking.

She found her by the central station. Nurse Smith. Nurse Smith. She called out. The head nurse was preparing meds for distribution.

That man doesn't talk. I ain't got time now to fool with his grunting; gotta pass out meds. Let me see, does he get anything now? Nope.

And Nurse Smith shuffled to the room at the other end of the hallway to begin distributing medications.

Whan go, whan go, whan go.

I can't understand you, Sweetie. What do you want?

Back and forth they went, the old man and the young woman. A janitor on the way to take the exit stairs passed by the two. He listened to their exchange for a couple of minutes then interjected, You'll never understand what he's saying. Then he opened the exit door and disappeared.

The young woman and the old man continued their frantic exchange. Realizing something was really bothering him and that he was trying to say something important, the young woman leaned over and addressed him face to face, almost exchanging breaths with him.

I'm trying to understand. What do you want, Sweetie? She put her hand on his shoulder. He turned his face away from her and stared at the wall opposite. He was trying to call up a vision of him sick and then him doing much better. Him playing cricket in Oronuevo and him eating pelau at Belle Isle. For a moment he was perplexed. What was happening to him? He slipped into a deep stillness to ponder yet again the smell of freshly turned funeral soil, so far from where his navel string was buried.

Finally, she remembered that he was wheeled to the window every day after lunch. Who knows how that ritual began, but he sat in that same spot almost daily beginning with the first winter he arrived, and then spring and summer and fall and winter and the other seasons again, and again once more, until he had marked a little over three years by the window. Through frost and snow and spring rains he watched out of it while he finished digesting his food. He followed the pedestrians heading to the liquor stores and other notable neighborhood destinations and absently glanced at cars crossing the Kercheval intersection on the way perhaps to Belle Isle? He contemplated navel strings and final resting places.

Maybe that's what he wanted now? she thought.

Do you want to go to the window, Sweetie?

Gratefully, the old man looked up at her and nodded. Finally, she understood and smiled back at him.

Now how to get him there, since she couldn't lift him by herself to put him in the wheelchair and everyone else was so busy. Conveniently, the one-ton white crane used to lift residents was already in a corner of the old man's room, likely in readiness for his afternoon window appointment. Luckily she had been trained to use it yesterday. So confidently she marched over to get it. With its boom pointed toward the floor she maneuvered the lift near the old man's bed and removed the halter left dangling on the hook. He was almost smiling as she leaned over him to place his arms through the halter, pull a strap between his legs, fasten it in the back, and check the placement of the loops for the hook.

Then she stood back to look at him.

You're a mess, Sweetie. At least let me wash your face. He nodded, a crooked little smile developing.

After she washed his face and combed his few strands of hair, she wheeled the chair by the bed and locked it into what she thought would be the perfect spot to receive the old man when she was ready to lower him.

She was almost ready with everything and then.

Oh my God, Sweetie. I bet your diaper needs changing. She rolled the wheelchair aside and unfastened the halter. His crooked little smile turned into a look of alarm.

Don't worry, Sweetie; I know what I'm doing, and she began to change and wash him with the adroitness of an old pro.

He closed his eyes at the feel of the young hand covered by a warm washcloth wiping Mummy's territory. There's nothing there anymore, Mummy. It's all gone.

With the halter and wheelchair back in place, she moved the crane into a position parallel to the bed. All of this activity occurred over and around the sunray, now angled slightly off the bed. The young woman darted in and out of its range as she prepared the crane without paying any attention to the motes traveling up and down the ray and the intermittent sunshine that caused her to squint. At last she felt the sun's warmth.

Hey, Sweetie, you're going to have a warm day at the window. You may not even be able to stand it.

She placed a pillow on the wheelchair seat for comfort and rolled him onto his side. Now she was ready. She turned the directional knob on the lever to move the boom up and pumped the lever until the boom reached a good level for hooking the halter. Then she slid the base of the crane under the bed and pumped again, gently lifting his once-hefty body off the bed, guiding it all the way. He was now almost facedown and moving his heavily wrinkled arms and thin legs as if he was winding up in the yard to bowl to Toli.

Hold on, Sweetie. Don't move so much. I'm going to roll you over to the chair. We don't have far to go; hang in. Oh you know what I mean.

He nodded, his smile having returned.

As she positioned the old man over the wheelchair, she pulled his legs down and around to make sure his bottom hit the chair first. She reached to change the directional knob so that she could now lower the boom when she pumped the lever. It was jammed. It wouldn't move at all, not to pump up, not to pump down.

Oh my God, what am I going to do? She looked up at Sweetie, who was moving his arms left over right and right over left, his legs in running formation, and said firmly, Be still until I figure this thing out.

She was able to reach the emergency cord by his bed and pulled and pulled and pulled. But no one came to the room. The room had no phone because no one ever called the old man. She began yelling.

Nurse Smith, Nurse Smith. Someone. Help.

No one came. All she heard were responses from other residents. We're here, they yelled out. One lady down the hall began screaming. The young staffer yelled back.

Everything is fine; don't worry.

So she patted the old man on his shoulder and said, Okay Sweetie, don't let them upset you. You're going for a ride now. And she rolled the entire contraption, Sweetie and all, over to the doorway and looked up and down the hall. No one, not a soul was in sight. She yelled again, Nurse Smith, Nurse Smith, someone.

No one.

The nursing station was midway down the hall. She thought to roll the crane to the station and use the phone to call for help, but the crane's pivot wheel suddenly locked tight. She pushed her foot on the wheel lock, then lifted up on it, then kicked it. She kneeled down to jiggle it, but it wouldn't loosen. So now the crane wouldn't move out of the room or back into it.

We're stuck, Sweetie. She smiled. He smiled, too, and nodded, but thought to himself, Man must live.

She realized she had to chance it at this point. He wasn't so high up in the air; things looked relatively stable if she could get him to keep absolutely still.

Sweetie, I have to call for help. You have to be real good and be still. Don't move your hands or feet. What are you doing anyway? You look like you're pitching in a baseball game. Be still; I'm going to call for help.

He hung there, his brown body against the white crane, and watched the young staffer rush down the hall.

Well maybe luck's allowed today, maybe, maybe. I'll be able to go to Belle Isle to see another game. Yeah, buddy, yeah. Yuh run with de bat when one guy hit de ball; he's going to run to try and score as many runs as he can. It depends on how hard yuh hit de ball. If yuh hit it real hard, it go over the boundary, that's a six. Yuh score big, den. If yuh don't reach to the end, they run yuh out, they call it runout; some of them bhais can't make it; they try to make one run and sometimes they don't; they don't make it den they want to make two runs, and so on, and when one guy hit the ball and he don't hit it hard enough and he hit it in front of one of the fielders and he have to run with the bat in he hand and he run, run, and what the hell. Yes buddy, run, run. She ran to the telephone, and in the instant she turned her head to grab the receiver, knocking over a silk floral arrangement in the process, and hit the button for security, she heard a loud snapping noise. Oh my God and she whipped her head around, expecting to see the old man on the floor.

But the crane was completely upright in the doorway and the boom in the same position she had left it. Only he was gone, halter and all. She froze, not able to respond when security finally answered the phone.

She ran over to the crane and passed her hand under where the old man should have been hanging. He really wasn't there. Sweetie, Sweetie, where are you? She squeezed past it to enter his room and looked under the covers, under the bed, in the closet, in the restroom. She ran from room to room; like a madwoman; residents called out to her, each with his or her own need for food, water, diaper, conversation.

Not now, she hollered back to them. Not now.

She pushed open the exit door. She ran down the stairs yelling, Old man, old man. She ran from floor to floor, past the floor staff, looking into each bedroom and each utility closet. When she returned to the fourth floor, Nurse Smith, the head of security, and most of the floor's staff were calmly standing by the lift, looking at her quizzically.

The old man is gone, Nurse Smith. He left.

What are you talking about?

He's just gone.

By this time the huddle of fourth-floor staff and a few from the other floors, along with the head of security, began prowling the halls, peering behind the nursing counter and into the other rooms searching for the old man. The head of security, a rather large, beefy man, tried to push the lift into the room, and when it wouldn't roll, he picked it up and moved it aside. Another staff member went to the wheelchair and shook it. This unnerved Nurse Smith, who yelled out, He ain't there, fool.

Bewildered, the young woman stood in the middle of the hallway in front of the old man's room. She began sobbing, long tears descending like a waterfall. Snot fell freely from her nose. She stared at the lift and at the wheelchair and at the bed and at the window in his room. It was then she remembered that the room was sunny before; now it was gray. She looked up and down the hall, and the whole place seemed gray. Didn't she tell the old man as she was preparing him for the crane that he would have a real sunny day at the window?

She walked slowly to the hall window, put her knee on the ledge, and peered up and down the Boulevard.

What the hell you looking for, girl? He damn sure ain't out there.

To the astonishment of the head nurse, the young woman, said, Hush, and squeezed her eyes enough to be able to peer through the bright sun. She looked up and down trying to spot the old man. The sun was coming from south, bright like a new beginning. Traffic was riding into it. But she saw nothing. No old man. She pushed her wet face against the window and stared openly into the sun.

Old man, how could you do this to me in my first week? I didn't want to stay here forever, but I need this job now. What have you done? They'll fire me for sure. How did I lose you? Why did you do this to me? I was trying to help you.

But if she had heard the commotion south of the nursing home, just inside the island on the north side of the Casino. If she had known the jubilation all of them there were experiencing as the last batsman hit the last ball in the last innings over, over, over the boundary so far it couldn't be recovered. All of the players stood with arms outstretched and knees slightly buckled, wonderment and joy on their faces; women and men spectators clutched their hearts, clutched each other, and clutched their children as they watched the ball's trajectory over the road, past the sun, over the river heading west and out of view. And then this tremendous release of clapping and crying and rummy shouts coming from the entire Casino area, pitch and oval, picnic benches, across the road over to the riverside. Had she heard the chorus, loud as one voice,

Well played, old bhai, well played, well played.

If she had heard all of that, she would have well understood.

Ole Year's Night

Shut your mouth, go away / Mama look a boo boo dey.

—From "Booboo Man" by Lord Melody, Trinidad, 1956

Just past midnight and the adults were finished with praying on their knees and wishing each and all a blessed New Year. The children were wet with parental kisses and embraces and incomprehensible predictions about the future from aunts, uncles, and family friends, most immediately about succeeding in the upcoming grade or even attaining a Dr. before their name. No one said anything like that to me, of course, about being a doctor or someone upscale, but I got a few warm hugs, as well, and felt the magic. Mostly because I was wearing a nice frilly dress and carried a little purse that contained a hanky, a small comb, and a pack of gum. That's all, but the purse was a sign of grown-upness. It was plain winter-black faux leather with a gold clip to lock it, and it had two handles that fit neatly over my thin arms. I wore black pumps, also faux, which I put on after removing my boots. My hair was well curled, likely from the paper twists Mummy used at Easter and at Ole Year's. Twice annually my hair received this paper curl treatment, including plenty slathering of rancid coconut oil direct from the islands. All of this would occur just after a good dose of castor oil to clean the system. My winter coat was from the year before, but Mummy, a well-respected seamstress in the community, had lengthened it, so it still fit this year. It would be years before anything I wore needed letting out width-wise. I left the purse on the bed in the room where all the other ladies left theirs. Occasionally I would visit the purse to dab my nose or refresh a curl, the kinds of things big ladies would do. I opened the gum and shoved a piece into my mouth, a kind of pre-souse palate cleansing. I was feeling strong for my nine years, yuh know, in tune with the adult excitement. Something was definitely in the air, and all present in Mistah Joseph's steamy and large lower eastside apartment were dedicated to fêting the night away, including me.

The trip over to the Joseph apartment from the various neighborhoods in Detroit—east, west, south, north, all over—was a difficult one that year for the assorted Islanders gathering for souse and dancing. The trees were laden with icicles and the roads were like ice-skating rinks. They nearly didn't make it to Mistah Joseph's. If you could only know how really cold and icy Detroit was that winter, especially for these people who were only freshly adapting to the climate. The men were better at engaging the weather, especially as they had to go out in it to work. My daddy worked at a gas station at the time; he was really out in the elements. The women more tended to hang on to sun and memories of it and beach excursions; few of them worked outside of the house. So for them, Detroit summers were easier to negotiate with their gardens, birds chirping and all. For them, winters were monstrous.

The ride over to Mistah Joseph's house was unbelievably slow. If it was anything like my family, all the daddies driving that night didn't recall any time before then that the roads had been so scary, as if they had been in Detroit for ages. They gripped their steering wheels, all the while commenting on how bad the driving, especially the side streets. Various Mummies, like mine, assured the car occupants that everything would be OK, Just take your time, Daddy. I wondered why my family was on the road in that kind of weather, but it was Ole Year's Night, after all, and who wanted to miss the fête at Mistah Joseph's? Not us. Not anyone. Not me. It was a big deal: the souse, meeting up with everyone all together, not just one by one occasionally throughout the year. It was a time to catch up as a group, exchange information about what was happening in the islands, some of which were slipping away from colonial control. The men gathered in corners to talk about that and pontificate over nips of scotch, the preferred drink of many island men—don't let them fool you about the rum and Coca Cola thing—about the leadership of each independence movement, what it meant, and so on, as if they would directly be affected anymore. After all, they were in Detroit. No independence movement here. They were just trying to make it in their new circumstances. That's all any of them were trying to accomplish. This Ole Year's, every Ole Year's, was the only party in their control, and the revelers would arrive almost as a cluster, no matter inclement weather.

The women discussed how their lives were going along. Oh, yes, there was a Missus Joseph, but she only intermittently appeared and not as a full participant in the fête. The women had a way of talking about her as if they knew her but then really didn't talk to her, except as pleasantries.

How you doing, Missus? Her name was Elizabeth, but hardly anyone addressed her as such, except for her sister-in-law.

Oh, I'm holding on, she would say. Yuh know. And she would look at you and hunch her back, shake her head, look down and begin rocking right there on the edge of the bed. I don't know what kind of information these ladies were deciphering from these few movements. Sometimes I think they faked understanding her for conversation's sake. Yuh know? But who was I to know then? Now, as I am grown, I have an idea that they understood more than I realized and knew how best to communicate with her.

No matter, she was a curiosity to me, a woman who couldn't handle her business. She didn't even cook. Where I got that notion back then that cooking was essential to being a woman is beyond me, since up to this day, cooking is not one of my favorite things to do, and to tell you the truth, I have a few dishes I can well organize, but I'd just as soon not. Cooking or not, house cleaning or not, you had to feel sorry for her. Something was wrong with her. All she could do was be sad. Given this basic understanding, the women and girls would always peep in on her just upon arrival. Her room was directly across from the room where the women put their purses and coats. That room was the spare where Mistah Joseph's sister, the woman they called Miss Nurse, slept sometimes after her shift at the hospital. She wasn't really a full nurse, but Miss Nurse worked at the hospital as some kind of an assistant. She knew a lot when you combined the modern medicine she learned from the hospital and old island remedies. So she was Miss Nurse to all of us and always dressed in white and always with a little smile. Maybe that's what she needed to deal with the patients in the hospital. But she was attentive to Missus Joseph, as well, whom she always called by her first name. Elizabeth, how yuh going along gyul? Not like us, useless and phony, at least in my opinion. She could really communicate with her sister-in-law, comb her hair, massage her neck, and hug her. I think she was the only one to make Missus Joseph laugh a real laugh. Yes, the only times I saw her laugh were when Miss Nurse came around. Elizabeth, tell me a little joke, nuh, and Missus Joseph would mumble something and Miss Nurse would laugh and I would wonder what the hell she said. What was the joke? But Mummy and the other women would laugh; so I would laugh as well.

Miss Nurse was an important member of the community. She at least could relate to Missus Joseph in a real way. Like my mother the seamstress, she was often called on by the community for assistance. When people needed clothing or mending, they called my mother. When they needed something medical, they would contact Miss Nurse before calling the doctor. Both of them possessed respected areas of expertise.

The men put their coats in Mistah Joseph's room, which was down the hall from his wife's. Remember, this apartment was the largest of the apartments they had lived in, and it was gorgeous. Missus Joseph would almost always be sitting on her bed rocking and then weakly move her mouth once we entered. I don't think it was an attempt at a smile, but an acknowledgement of our presence or maybe an attempt to communicate. The women and their daughters would go into the bedroom where Missus Joseph lived and try to comfort her craziness. Even the little girls knew that something was wrong with her. She was a frail, gray-haired, wrinkled woman with very dark skin, but not as dark

as the Mistah. He was tall and round-headed and bald. His stomach
bulged over the belt, and he always had a stogie in his mouth. Who
knows how he ate the souse or anything for that matter, considering
the stogie and all. But he was jolly and full of laughter. To this day I
don't know his job of work, how he made his living. Even years later,
after Missus Joseph had died and Daddy and I would go visit him, I
couldn't figure out his line of work. And, of course, you wouldn't ask
that kind of thing, even of my father. It would be inappropriate.

When we peeped in on the Missus, she would only talk about
her head hurting and her beautiful home near the beach back in
the islands and how she was stolen away from there and brought
to this country. I would sit on the bed on the other side of her from
Mummy. Sometimes when Missus Joseph was too weird, I would sit
by Mummy and lean over to listen. Mummy would offer advice about
this and that, how to tie head with Limacol or the best way to lock
up things from tief, because Missus Joseph always complained about
tief coming for her jewelry. Now and again Mistah Joseph would pass
by the bedroom door and shake his head. You could see that he was
sad, but there was nothing he could do. Now and again you would
catch a conversation between the men and women about her. Still, it
was difficult to fathom why she spoke only to the women who came
to see her in the bedroom and why she didn't come out to join the
fête. Even after the Ole Year passed she kept in her room. It smelled
musty in there but not stink, just thick and close with problems. Her
hair was always in gray, crinkly braids. The ladies would stop in one
by one, sometimes two at a time to wish Missus Joseph Happy New
Year. But by this time, I was always too caught up in the excitement
of a whole year gone by and a new one arriving. Especially that year

because some new cute boys were among the guests, and the girls were already vying for their attention.

However long it took the revelers to greet the New Year, probably no more than fifteen minutes by my sense of time after someone—I don't know to this day who announced the ball dropped, and I don't know how they knew since no TV was on—everyone exclaimed excitement about the calendar change, the pot cover lifted, and fragrance from the souse escaped and made its way to a large, almost bare room that maybe was the dining room, but for tonight it was going to be the dance floor. Only a couch in a corner by a window and a few folding chairs provided sit-down huddle space for the children who had come with their parents and would be lucky enough to stay up for the whole night, or as long as their parents remained at Mistah Joseph's. You could feel the excitement, the change of time, the possibility of new, the hope. Except for Missus Joseph. You were never sure if she understood what was happening. I always felt a little sadness somewhere as the New Year became more of a fact, after that initial excitement because I could feel her loneliness and lostness as if she was sitting on my shoulder. Like she was trapped between here and there or something like that, not with us but not gone.

Maybe about an hour before the New Year kicked the old one out, a crew of adults would huddle over the pot of pig feet to determine the next step: when to convert the feet that had been cooking on slow fire for hours into souse. They had to figure the logistics of moving pig feet through a series of clear water rinses and the exact right moment to add the onions, green pepper, and cucumbers. Then the delight of biscuits, the kind that came in the packs that you shoved into the oven for a few minutes. The biscuits had to be hot, hot, butter dripping, even though the souse was cold at serving. It was in this process that the adults reacquainted themselves after a year away from the group. Too, there might be new fellow travelers for the evening. The children, as well, tried to figure out who was who. It wasn't easy to sort each other out because some parents were not consistent in coming to the Ole Year's night fête. You may see the child as a baby, and then several years later when it was talking in full sentences and then when it was almost high-school age. To the best of my knowledge I don't think the Josephs ever had a child. But you never know how these things go. I used to hear a rumor about Mistah Joseph having a son. He may have been at one of the parties. By the time I reached the age of better wisdom than I had the night in question, I still wouldn't have asked for those kinds of particulars. It wouldn't have been appropriate.

My parents and I were regulars. Every year we were wherever the fête was, no matter the apartment Mistah Joseph and his wife were living in. They changed a few times over the years from a dingy two-bedroom place to this final place for Ole Year's, a large three-bedroom with lots of windows and wood trim and wood floors and a big enough space for real dancing. That was where I danced for the first time ever with a man, Mistah Joseph, because Daddy didn't dance, and, of course, I was too young for boys.

Once the pot cover came off the pig feet, it was almost time to fête and for the real magic to begin. Now the adults moved as a gaggle. Soon bowls of souse and biscuit appeared out of nowhere, landing in the hands of the children, who were settled into the corner couch and folding chairs. Then the adults reassembled in the kitchen for additional shots of scotch for the New Year and to dish out souse for themselves. Each year they fussed over the quality of the pot and each year voted it excellent by the depth of their bowls. The children were left on their own in the living room. That year none of the children really knew each other, but the older ones struck up conversations about the usual topic, school or a movie or a song. I usually didn't know much about the American songs or movies. My family only listened to calypso and Tito Puente. They didn't allow me to go to many movies.

In my humble opinion, there is no smell like the smell of souse. The combination of lime, cucumber, and raw onions overtakes the freshness of the pig feet. And then the texture of the feet stiffens in reaction to the lime (some use vinegar, most in fact, but Mistah Joseph also added lime, which I have grown to prefer), while the bones are curiously soft and responsive to chomping and sucking after the meat is gone. To this day, it is still one of my favorite foods, especially with the hot biscuits that come a dozen in a pack. I think back then they were made by Wonder Bread.

We were settled with our bowls of souse when one of the cute boys raised a piece of meat on his fork and screwed up his face. I thought to myself that he must not like the feet; he didn't look islander anyway. So I immediately concluded that he was scorning the food. I was ready to scorn him, even though he was the cutest of the crop, when I noticed something slimy dangling from the meat he held up. Now pig feet can by messy and sticky when first cooked, but the sousing process eliminates that. So I truly was confused by the slime until the boy said, Ugh my brother sneezed. I don't know that I would have responded with humor if someone had blown snot onto my food, but laughter it was from all the rest. Not me. I was horrified and wondering what would happen next. We all sat there, them laughing, me not, until the boy's mother came over, retrieved the nastiness, and replaced it with a fresh bowl. By this time the moment was spoiled. I couldn't properly eat the souse or enjoy the company of the other children. The cute boy wasn't cute anymore, and I was just trying to get away from this crew.

Eating finished and soon calypso took over. By this time another few shots had passed lips, and the predictions about the status of island politics grew even more furious. Mistah Joseph had all the hot tunes and all the calypsonians to sing them: Kitchener, Invader, Sparrow. The first strains of music began to take over a few bodies. My mother was among those moving. Daddy didn't dance, but she did. She danced when cooking, when washing dishes, when cleaning house. It was she who got me into dancing. I think this is how she put herself back home, through moving to the music. Soon a little enclave of women began to shuffle and swish around, their slippers (you always brought some kind of flat shoes to replace the boots and for dancing) making a rhythm on the wood floor. Now I was wandering between the women and shifting my bottom as they did and moving my legs side to side. When the music took a break, I decided to visit my purse again, freshen up, and grab a stick of gum. O Lawd, no gum. I was confused. What happened to my gum? A few women were in the bedroom, one of them with her three-year-old daughter, who was clutching the remains of my pack of gum in her hand as she chewed away on a stick. Look, I was horrified. This was worse than slime on pig feet souse. I didn't know what to do, especially as this little chupid girl was grinning like a pig, happy with her tiefing and oblivious to my consternation. If you could only know instant hate as I felt it then. Instant, instant. I wanted to choke the little girl. I wanted to yell like murder. And most of all, I was hurt and felt violated. I felt powerless. I went by my mother on the dance floor still, and whispered, She take muh gum, that girl over there. I don't think Mummy quite heard me, especially as the woman with her offending daughter came over to speak to Mummy just then. They were Islanders. I could tell by the accent, small island. They began laughing and talking about what I don't know. By this time I had shut down, especially as the music had stopped while someone changed the record. I was disconsolate; the party was over for me.

You could feel the intensity of the atmosphere in the short break from dancing. I don't know quite how to describe it, but the place was really steamy and the smell of souse pervading. Everyone was smiling except me and, I suppose, Missus Joseph. I think that now, but then I didn't care one bit about smiling or her misery, only my gum and this little chupid girl in my purse. Then the music started up again. People were dancing and I was in the middle of the floor feeling lost. I can only imagine how my face must have looked angry. From nowhere Mistah Joseph, stogie and all, came over and bent low in front of me. May I have this dance? His voice was always low and slow, small island with a bit of rasp, maybe from the stogie and scotch. I didn't know how to respond when he held his hands out, but I took them. He was a giant in every way compared to me, for sure. He smiled and I couldn't help smiling back. I understood that I was going to experience something beyond a damn missing pack of gum. The music began. It wasn't the first time I heard the Booboo Man song. We would get the calypso tunes whenever someone went home and brought them back. "Booboo

Man" lingered in our Detroit community maybe longer than over there, maybe because we had to hold on to everything that came our way from back home. They could refresh over there with each Carnival. We had no Calypso Lords to make sense of Detroit.

Lord Melody—there were so many Lords over there interpreting the culture—but this Lord began

> *I wonder why nobody don't like me*
> *Or is it a fact that I'm ugly?*
> *I wonder why nobody don't like me*
> *Or is it a fact that I'm ugly?*

And you could feel the sway, but under these new circumstances, my hands held high by a giant, I couldn't quite figure out how to move my body. He moved one leg and the other in time and I followed. You can well imagine my arms by my neck; I was almost not breathing while trying to follow. Soon Mistah Joseph was gone from me, his eyes closed, big smile on the face and stogie hanging loose. The room was shuffling along, except Daddy and a few others. The floor was thick with feet brushing the wood. I didn't look for anyone anymore, not the cute boy, not the chupid girl, not Mummy. Not Daddy. Then we arrived at the chorus.

> *Mama look a booboo, they shout*
> *Their mother told them, Shut up your mouth*
> *That is your daddy. Oh no, my daddy can't be ugly so.*
> *Shut your mouth, go away*
> *Mama look a booboo dey.*

There's a point in the song when the band sings pampalam or something like that. And the whole contingent of Lord Melody dancers on the lower east side of Detroit were pampalamming and now stomping their way into the second stanza of the song.

I couldn't even digest my supper
Due to the children's behavior

By this time I was in full swing. I had found my legs, skinny as they were, and was well meeting the rhythm of "Booboo Man." All my frilly dress flipping from thigh to thigh and curls flopping from right side of head to next side were in full orchestration. You see the song starts out slow and ends fast so I had time to rev myself up. By the time we reached to the next chorus of shut your mouth, Miss Nurse was on the dance floor moving her arms up and down with a big smile on her face and her eyes well closed. Mummy, of course, was in another world. She had a scarf—I don't know to this day where she got it from, maybe it was the one she wrapped her neck with against the cold —and used it to connect her hands above her head in full mas mode, like she was parading round the Savannah in Port of Spain. I could feel the music lifting my feet left and right. And at the last chorus everyone, even those off to the side, even Daddy because he loved to sing, everyone in that room sang to the top:

Shut your mouth, go away
Mama look a booboo dey.

Then the record stopped, but the singing continued:

Shut your mouth, go away
Mama look a booboo dey

And they continued and continued gently stomping all of them and me singing till my lungs could barely push out another note, and I was laughing so hard and Mistah Joseph had somehow gotten rid of the stogie without me noticing. Mummy and several other women were right close pampalamming. Everyone was moving. I looked over to see what Daddy was doing and here he was dancing with Miss Nurse. O Lawd, how did that happen? You know how you can be taken with surprise to see your daddy dancing with another woman? I don't know if could say I was amused or what, especially since neither of them could really dance. Miss Nurse was jerky with her movements and comical, her eyes closed and head nodding as if she was giving a lecture. Daddy was even funnier because he had a big belly, and I think that's all that was moving, and he was going up and down on his toes and shifting the belly side to side. It's difficult to explain, but look, in the final analysis I was happy. My mother was dancing away and so was Miss Nurse. You could see joy in her face. And surprise of all, Missus Joseph was leaning against the door to her bedroom, which was right off the living room; so she could see everything. She was leaning and smiling with head nodding in time to the music. I'm pampalamming myself, left foot then right stomping, wondering if people in the streets could hear us with our pampalam pampalam. Daddy and Miss Nurse were right by Mistah Joseph and me, moving the same as we. I think everyone noticed Missus Joseph at the same time, and their feet stomped even harder, and hands clapped to the pampalam, except for mine because I was still holding on to Mistah

Joseph for dear life. Except for the Missus because she was leaning against her door all by herself laughing, yes, laughing. And except for Miss Nurse because she was holding on to my daddy's hands. He had a serious look on his face because he never danced. This was the one and only time ever I saw him move to any kind of music ever, except for when he swayed to his singing, but that doesn't count as dancing. To this day I wonder why he was dancing with Missus Joseph and not with Mummy. But Mummy wasn't clapping either because of the scarf and her hands in the air and stomping like she was trying to wake up some booboo man jumbie somewhere. Oh, even maybe she found herself back home right then.

Who knows how these kinds of fêtes end? The music stops but the rhythm lingers, for whatever remaining pig feet to dance in the pot. The ride home for my family was fun and fine, no worries for as long as I was awake, but days later Mummy and Daddy rehashed the evening, amazed at Missus Joseph. My family takes everything as a sign of something. So, I think they spent weeks evaluating every moment of that Ole Year's night for a signal about the times. You know what I mean? How would politics go back home? What would happen with us here? And all of it had to do with Missus Joseph coming out of her room and participating even at that level for the first time ever as far as we knew.

No matter how the adults would later interpret that moment, I understood something else. Because at the most profound booboo chorus, when pampalamming was at its height and the wood floors were vibrating and the whole lower east side of the city was melting from Lord Melody in full swing, just then I noticed the little chupid girl sitting in the corner with her lips poked out and tears forming in her eyes. My feet continued to stomp right left, right left in time to "Booboo Man." Chupid little girl, I said to myself, I'm dancing; look at you. Now that I look in hindsight, she was probably sleepy. She was so young, not like me. What did she know of souse and dancing? She didn't know about weather. She didn't know about the ice and snot that night in the city. Still, I threw my most wicked, wicked grin over by her just as everyone was stomping on the last line of booboo dey. Even now I tell myself, good for you.

Love in the Dollar Store

How he met that angel of a woman was pure fate come to save his life from heading south, meaning it was tanking, falling apart—nowhere to run, nowhere to hide. Felipe was beyond loser, beyond a totally useless piece-of-shit idiot, beyond all redemption for that matter. He was on the skids to oblivion, the midnight express to nowhere. In the vernacular of Detroit speak: he was through, done for. True, on one level he understood that about himself. But on another he almost always projected bravado, handsome hope, a winning gold-laced smile. Wow, meeting Dhal flipped Felipe 180 degrees from looking down to looking skyward with the hope that he might begin to mean something to someone and the possibility that he could finally unite the Felipe that traversed Detroit streets with whatever of him was still geographically south south south, floating somewhere in the Caribbean. It was a crazy time for Felipe and for Dhal, too, a real turn of events that propelled their lives in totally different directions as they moved into the new century. Well for Felipe maybe not a turn of events, more like a kick to the flywheel of his failed life, helping him to restart his engine, reorganize his plans, and move on down the road. Here's what happened.

The EZ Dollar Store was especially crowded on the morning of August 26, 1998, a Wednesday in the last week before Labor Day and the beginning of the school year. Mothers were in full swing shopping for back-to-school supplies for their kindergarten and elementary children. So this rush of high-energy shoppers on a Detroit hump day, when the city tended to wind down in preparation for the weekend, didn't portend well for the feet and patience of the store clerks, but suggested many dollars for the store owner. Kids in tow, mothers picked over the athletic socks and packs of assorted panties for girls and underwear for boys on the racks to the left of the store as you entered the door. Of all of the dollar stores on the northwest side of Detroit, EZ contained the widest variety of treasures and was the best stocked with basic garments, artistic supplies, tools, soaps, bleaches, wine glasses, and dishes of any store for miles around.

But it was intimately small and not air conditioned so the front door, propped open that morning to vent the heat, only allowed in more, plus bugs. And the day was truly hot and steamy, even by Detroit standards where air, no matter the temperature, got trapped between buildings high and low and mixed with auto fumes, garbage odors, and the smell of its people moving from one place to the other. Even in the neighborhoods that had reverted to farmland on the east side, the air covered the terrain like a heavy blanket of despair. Now that was in the heart of the city. In the suburbs, things may have been a bit cooler, the grass greener, the parade of people thinner, buildings cleaner, and so on. But everywhere in the real Detroit, a peculiar funk covered everything, even the river.

In this case, funk didn't mean stink; it meant odiferous with all the above mentioned nostril-tickling gases plus bar-b-q, barbacoa, and shish kabob. But you get the picture, the same way of saying the same thing and eating it, too. For this story also we must add roti and curry. No mind, it's humanity upon humanity wondering how in the hell they all landed in a city hailed for its industrial innovations and car factories, producing vehicles for earthly travel, and its churches, fabricating ways to reach the great beyond in high style, having secured earthly riches from an accumulation of hot and cold blest days.

Almost anyone—meaning the factory workers (unionized and non-unionized), the bread makers, the hot dog venders, the sanitation workers, the household workers, the landscapers, construction workers (unionized and non), veterinarians and staff, and dollar-store clerks—almost anyone of that ilk who survives Detroit deserves heaven. We won't worry just now about the eternal homes of some of those whose names line the city's streets. Let's just say that the chances of them living in gorgeous mansions in the beyond are slim to none. But commoners who benefited in however meager ways from the crumbs that spilled from the back doors of the earthly mansions of the Detroit rich, well, they've got to be heaven bound.

And there was a shipload of them in EZ just then, all on the righteous path to our lord in the sky just because we are all poor. What bullshit, thought Dhal as she scurried from one end of the store to the other finding crayons, then socks, then nail polish (the mothers need something for themselves), and because not only mothers shopped, a bag full of kitchen utensils for a couple, stacking up on household supplies such as wastebaskets, sponges, cleaning fluids, and so on.

She: Hey Sweetheart, look at these cloth napkin and tablecloth sets. Wouldn't they look beautiful in our new living room? He: Oh, Baby, you know you're the decorating genius. Get what you want.

Oh brother, thinks Dhal, how long will this lovey dovey stuff last? Absolutely, Sweetheart, and Baby, the sky is the limit. Get what you want. After all, you are in a dollar store.

Being a dollar-store devotee herself, Dhal well appreciated the savings and occasional quality if you picked over the items carefully enough. Since beginning employment at EZ in March, she had been able to decorate her bedroom in her Aunt Tantan's house in fine style down to the last pink, frilly detail thanks to EZ and had helped tidy her aunt's general living quarters, especially the sewing room and kitchen, with an assortment of EZ plastic containers and interlocking shelving. There was no hope for the aunt's bedroom as she kept it cluttered with Vincie artifacts, a few articles of his clothing, including a suit rack with his brown suit—she buried him in the black one—some mementos she had kept from various restaurant excursions, a fan from Stanley's Chinese, and so on.

It was the kind of day when Dhal didn't know whether to cry or laugh, praise the Detroit Lawd or curse the assortment of Hindu gods and customs she left back in Tesoro. This kind of oppressive heat without the surrounding sea confused her, making her feel more trapped than the cold winter she had just experienced for the first time. Then again, she was working, making a few Yankee bucks, free from the even more oppressive constrictions of life with her Tesoro family. This jumble of thoughts swished and swooshed back and forth in her cranial cavity as she rocked and rolled her way through EZ's aisles secretly hoping that the store's door would miraculously slam shut to any additional customers until the current crew cleared out. But a relatively short, muscular (and good-looking) man slipped in.

It was Felipe. He stood just by the door trying to get the lay of the store when he spotted Dhal running from one customer to the other. She didn't notice him at all, but for him all further movement stopped. He couldn't believe his eyes. She passed in front of him once or twice again, just enough for him to load up his lungs with her powdery fragrance. They expanded with the sweetness and he became lightheaded, his eyes clouding over as he was forgetting to breathe out. He knew right off the bat that on a scale of one to ten, she was over the top. Soon he was near drooling, his tongue beginning to dangle lecherously past his lips, and sensations beginning to heat up in the southern regions of his body. In short, he went bazodee, quickly becoming weak and helpless and chupid for so. Plus, he had the silliest grin on his face when Farouq at the counter asked if he could be of some help.

Just looking around man; thank you. That short exchange with Farouq brought him somewhat back to his senses. Felipe made a move the next time Dhal swept past him. Her beauty had brought out the rogue in him.

Miss, I need a birthday balloon. The kind you blow up with helium.

She stopped dead in her tracks as her ears tuned in to his accent. Then the big bling medallion hanging around his neck on a thick gold chain caught her eye. Well, sir, we have a large variety right there in front. The gentleman behind the counter would be glad to help you.

Thank you.

And he meandered off toward the back of the store to regroup, leaving her to stare at him from the front of aisle one until a woman approached her with a question about trouser socks. He found himself in the section of workmen's gloves and bags of cleanup rags, the real reason he had spontaneously stopped into the store in the first place. It was his first time at that store even though he, too, shopped regularly at dollar stores as he encountered them throughout the city. He had become a meanderer in life, wandering from one city to the next, one city block to the next and from one corner to the next in the various apartments and rooming houses he had inhabited. His feet and hands were ever restless in response to mental signals firing at nonstop dazzling speeds.

Dhal passed him nearly half an hour later fiddling with electrical doodads on the rack just over from an assortment of pliers and screwdrivers. What is he looking for now? He turned around and flashed a wide, toothy smile revealing small, even teeth, the four in front thinly framed with gold. Not bad, she thought. The mouth is clean, but the gold is old. The medallion is way too much. I wonder where he is from.

Then she became deeply engaged with a young mother and her five-year-old who were studying some little hard plastic purses with double handles that flipped up and down and snapped in the middle for closure. For only a dollar, the purses came loaded with pink-and-blue hard, flat sour candy with little messages of encouragement written in red: *you go girl* or *play to win*.

Now see, Dhal encouraged the mother, these little candies give messages that are important for little girls to learn very early on.

That's true.

Does she read yet?

She knows her alphabet.

Well, you can use these candies to help her along with her reading. Every time she wants one, make her read the inscription before giving it to her. And Dhal smiled broadly at the child. You go girl!

The little girl said out loud so nearly the entire store could hear, Mama, that lady talks funny.

The mother began apologizing profusely, but Dhal was well used to people's reactions to her accent, and she herself often had to talk her way through her inability to understand the combination of Midwest and South that dominated the tongues on her side of town. Not to worry, Mum, Dhal assured the lady.

Then the girl, dressed in denim short pants and a red midriff and oblivious to her social faux pas, sang, Go go and began to do a little dance in her flopping white sandals in front of the toy rack where the pink purses hung opposite shelves of plastic food wraps and garbage bags.

The sale was a done deal.

Next Dhal encountered a woman, maybe in her fifties, reviewing the plastic containers on a shelf in aisle three. Dhal was working like a whirling dervish that day because Laila, the other lady on the floor, was off taking care of some immigration business—she was at the next step of becoming a permanent resident—and only Dhal, Farouq at the counter, and Benny on stock would hold down the fort until Laila's return tomorrow. May I help you, Mum?

I'm looking for something to store my cornmeal in.

Do you keep a lot or a little on hand?

Oh I keep a lot because I does use it to make coo-coo.

Where yuh from, nuh, Mum?

I'm from de islands.

Which one? I'm from over that way, too, from Tesoro.

Oh? I'm from Saint Catherine's. How nice to meet a Tesoran here.

Not many of you have reached quite this far.

Oh there are a few of us. Do you know my auntie?

And so the conversation went, with promises to stay in touch and a sale of several plastic containers for everything from cornmeal to socks.

You're very good, said the smiling, muscular man with the gold-rimmed teeth. He sidled up to Dhal after the woman from Saint Catherine moved on to the front counter to pay. Maybe you can sell me something.

You look like you're doing fine locating everything. Is there something else you need?

Well, I mentioned before I need a birthday balloon.

And I didn't see you up front looking for any.

Oh I know exactly which one I want. The blue and silver one over there with the red squiggles on the border and the message: Happy Birthday Baby.

That balloon was not among the assortment of balloons that dangled over Farouq's head, most of which were also of the happy birthday variety and with enough crazy messages to please anyone. But the muscular man wanted the one balloon that was not with the gaggle hanging already inflated or within easy reach of Farouq's long arm.

No, he wanted the one balloon that hung flattened, two balloons in above the rack against the wall in aisle six on the left side of the store. Dhal would have had to climb the ladder to retrieve the Happy

Birthday Baby, uninflated greeting in blue and silver with red squiggles on the border. So she did what came naturally to her.

Mr. . . .

Call me Felipe.

Mr. Felipe, depending on who you are buying this for . . .

It's for a very nice and beautiful young lady.

Well, the yellow balloon over there is very popular this time of year, especially for young ladies. Yellow for sun, you know. Plus yellow represents happiness and a loving and caring nature.

No, I have my heart set on the blue and silver one over there with the red squiggles on the border.

That's so masculine.

She's a very strong woman.

All righty then. And with that Dhal proceeded to do what she also knew how to do well—stall. She went in search of a ladder to reach the top because the long mechanical fingers could possibly tear the balloon from where it was taped to the wall.

Just a minute, Mr. Sir, I'll be right back.

Of course, on the way to find the ladder, she ran across three or four customers she practically threw herself at with offers of assistance. Mum, let me help you find this or that. Sir, we have a fine selection of screwdrivers over here. Oh Miss, kitchen strainers are on the shelf in aisle three. Come let me show you; we have metal and plastic. Personally, I prefer the plastic because it's quieter, and we have a fabulous selection of colors. Look, these reds just came in, and we have bowls to match.

In this way she killed at least half an hour in aisles one through four, hoping that the man in aisle six would go away or settle for a more easily accessible balloon. No luck for Dhal that day. By the time she escorted a woman looking for fabric softener to the counter, Mr. Felipe met her there with a big grin on his face.

I still want that balloon.

So Dhal found the ladder and began her ascent with Felipe watching every movement of her butt cheeks—left up and right up, left up and right up—and checking out the firmness of her calves as she mounted each step. Not bad, he thought. I wonder where she is from?

Dhal passed by the athletic socks and the trouser pants socks and the little thin thin nylon ankle socks with loud colors and abstract designs (very fashionable with the young crowd) when a balloon Farouq had been inflating—this one saying just plain congratulations with some multicolored representations of balloons on the front of the main balloon, which was black—well Farouq's balloon escaped and shot past Dhal like a bullet, completely surprising her and throwing her off balance.

She lost control of the ladder, which began flipping backward away from the wall. Farouq saw what was happening and began running past the boxes hemming him in at the counter (there had just been a new shipment of dish towels he was trying to inventory from his workstation since Laila wasn't there that day). Oh my Dolly. Oh Dolly. And he tripped face forward into a pile of the towels, while knocking over a few of the also newly arrived bamboo good luck money plants. Fortunately, they didn't have water in them yet.

Customers gathered in the area to see if they could help. They began gasping almost in unison. Benny came running to the front with a box cutter still in his hand and pushed his way to the scene. The store clients looked on in horror. The young couple held each other's hands for dear life. The little girl began crying while her mother, trapped in the crowd, could only bury her daughter's face in her leg.

More than her life flashed in front of Dhal; the store's ceiling passed before her with an uncanny unfamiliarity. She never had realized it was actually a drop ceiling and that things were stored up there. White T-shirts? Tablecloths?

Then time stood still for her even as the ladder rushed to meet the shelves of trash bags. Remember, although the store's ceiling was high, the floor space was really limited. How it managed to house six aisles was a miracle. Dhal's back would have hit the shelf and who knows what would have happened to her, except that her body slackened as she fainted and lost her grip on the ladder. This was a good thing because Felipe stood below at just that moment and caught her in his arms. Like in the movies, he caught her full, her upper torso nestled in his right arm, her body draped across his chest, and her legs dangled safely over his left arm. The ladder lodged against the shelves, forming a cozy hutch over the two.

The entire store erupted in hoots of glee. Everyone began slapping each other on the back and hugging and crying. Then all fell silent as Dhal opened her eyes suddenly in shock now to be in the arms of a man, any man, but this one smelled pretty good.

Hello, Dolly. When's your birthday?

She knew immediately it had been a mistake to not follow through with her original plan and use her given name at the job. Farouq had taken to calling her Dolly, and variations on the name abounded among customers and the store staff. But coming from this man's gold teeth while she was in his arms, Dolly sounded dangerous.

My name is not Dolly. Put me down please.

No thank you for saving your life? His lip edges now curled down, faking a scowl.

At this Dhal sighed in exasperation, wanting to give him a real piece of her mind.

By this time, Farouq had extricated himself from the towels and the good-luck bamboo plants. He grimaced at Felipe, climbed the ladder, retrieved the balloon, and inflated it back at the counter. Felipe, returning Farouq's stare, pulled a wad out of his right front jeans pocket and was just about to pay for all of his items when he asked Farouq to throw in one of the bamboo plants already on display.

Business concluded, Felipe walked out of the store with the balloon bobbing behind him and her eyes on his back. Then with unexpected and inexplicable joy in his heart, he reached his hand up and released the blue and silver happy birthday balloon to the Detroit August sky and watched until its red squiggles danced toward the sun and disappeared.